A FRIEND IN THE POLICE

A FRIEND
IN THE POLICE

John Givens

HARCOURT BRACE JOVANOVICH, *New York and London*

Requests for permission to make copies of
any part of the work should be mailed to:
Permissions, Harcourt Brace Jovanovich, Inc.
757 Third Avenue, New York, N.Y. 10017

Printed in the United States of America

LIBRARY OF CONGRESS CATALOGING IN PUBLICATION DATA
Givens, John.
A friend in the police.
I. Title.
PZ3.G4519Fr   [PS3557.I85]   813'.5'4   79-1822
ISBN 0-15-133538-9

First edition

B   C   D   E

A FRIEND IN THE POLICE

one)((÷)((÷)((÷)((÷)((÷)((÷)((÷)((÷)((÷)((÷)((÷)((÷)((÷)((÷)((÷)((

Heart? But Detective Sergeant Xlong was a man of true feelings, no matter how deeply he suppressed them. There were moments—they came upon him unexpectedly—when he would have kissed his fist had there been no regulation in the police handbook specifically discouraging public displays of emotion.

And it was true that, in a moment of self-consciousness, he had positioned the polished visor of his police cap at an angle so severe as to impair normal vision. But was he alone at fault? He thought not. Shouldn't the foreigner have cooperated? Of course he should. George Bates could have accepted the uncertainty of members of the police. There was no reason for their brief ritual to have limped. It could have soared.

"Your purpose for wishing to enter this country?"

Mr. Bates regarded the policeman calmly. He had come for his son. He didn't mention that Philip had been declared persona non grata and was evidently in danger of detention. Apparently he was determined to volunteer no information.

This did not surprise Detective Sergeant Xlong. There was a chill to the man, like mornings when river mists blotted out the sun.

George Bates had tried to make the necessary arrangements from his home in Los Angeles. He had been unable to accomplish anything. There was no American consulate here; nor was there any kind of trade office or information service that could act as an intermediary. Mr. Bates's attorney had a connection in the State Department, but there had simply been no string to pull. He was on his own.

"Then you are not a tourist?"

Instead of answering, George Bates rearranged his luggage on the inspection table and clicked open the locks. A crushing humidity radiated from the jungle. The planks beneath his feet were pocked with pools of decay. A pair of militiamen under the command of a junior officer blocked the door of the customs shed.

Detective Sergeant Xlong drummed his fingers on a pile of soggy documents. Pits gouged by the pointed sticks of childhood had healed imperfectly, giving his face the haphazard appearance of one comfortable with sudden violence.

"That is my declaration among those papers you have there before you."

The *Longevity* hove listlessly against the dock, her steel plates groaning with remorse. George Bates had been the only passenger to disembark. Had he wondered at that? There would have been no indication that the little coastal steamer planned to touch another port in the Archipelago, yet the other passengers remained on board.

"This visa is a tourist visa," the detective sergeant said, tossing down the passport.

"That's correct."

"You have been here before on a tour?"

George Bates looked steadily at the policeman but didn't reply.

"But of course there would have been an entry stamp, and an exit stamp, and other stamps; assuming, for the moment, you had crossed the frontier legally."

Mr. Bates still said nothing.

The detective sergeant sighed. He appeared to be puzzled by the irregular documents. Turning to consult a sheaf of greasy notices impaled on a spike above the desk, he asked an incoherent question.

Mr. Bates ignored him, hoping, perhaps, to imply he was not to be intimidated. Perspiration soaked his shirt. He obviously wanted to get past the formalities as quickly as possible.

The junior officer stepped forward and made a move to examine the passport, but Detective Sergeant Xlong halted him with a sharp grunt.

"What is your occupation?"

"I'm retired."

"You are married?"

"My wife is deceased."

The detective sergeant nodded as if he had expected as much. Mr. Bates's lips pressed tightly together.

"So you travel alone?"

George Bates glanced behind him. Except for some

bales of jute fiber and a broken crate of rotten fruit, the customs shed was deserted.

"This visa . . ." the junior officer began, but was again silenced.

"Mr. Bates, do you have the correct visa?"

"As you can see, it's stamped in my passport."

"Do you mean this visa?" The detective sergeant made no move to touch the passport. His left hand plunged into the webby armpit of his police shirt. "Why do you think this is the correct visa?"

"I got it at your consulate in Singapore no more than five days ago."

"Five days!" the junior officer repeated mockingly.

Detective Sergeant Xlong continued to pluck around the damp perimeter of his underarm, unable to trap whatever had attacked him. He bent to examine the empty pages of the addendum section in the back of the passport, at one point even scraping away a patch of mildew to peer beneath it in a gesture of painstaking justice.

"Perhaps you would like to visit some of the ruins?" the detective sergeant offered. "Take a few photographs? Buy some souvenirs?"

George Bates said he would not.

Detective Sergeant Xlong raised his head until he could see from beneath the bill of his cap. The skin around his eyes was as scarred as his cheeks and throat. "This needs a validation stamp," he said slowly. "You have a tourist visa, but you are not a tourist."

"No tourist!" echoed the junior officer. He began fumbling with his wet holster.

Mr. Bates still made no reply. His son had written of

harassment. The customs official, the immigration official, the officials from the National Police—although each branch had its characteristic methodologies, there wasn't a member of any of them whose hand couldn't find another's pocket as quickly as his own.

"You've neglected to receive the validation stamp."

George Bates gazed out the window. Warm sea swells gathered into gray waves that collapsed upon the beach. The junior officer had drawn his pistol, but at a word from his superior, he reholstered it and grudgingly moved to the far end of the customs shed.

Detective Sergeant Xlong observed George Bates curiously. He suspected that the American considered himself perfectly capable of regulating his emotions. Mr. Bates would take pride in coolness. He had rushed across half the world's time zones only to drag down the length of the Archipelago on a steamer clearly in no hurry to arrive anywhere. He would not have complained or betrayed indignation. He would have established his position on the rail of the *Longevity*, attended to the monotonous smear of jungle coastline, and held himself aloof. Good. Mr. Bates was patient. The detective sergeant would never disapprove of such behavior. He too was patient.

"It could have been simple. An afternoon in the ruins, a few photographs . . ."

"I haven't the time. And I didn't bring a camera."

"Then you must have the validation stamp. Without it, this visa is useless."

Detective Sergeant Xlong glanced at his junior officer, who was stalking back and forth at the far end of the shed, obviously disappointed. He hated being excluded. At this stage of his career, however, he might benefit from a sense of loss.

"I wasn't told in Singapore I'd need such a stamp."

"In Singapore"—the policeman smiled, fingering the wedge of scar tissue on his cheek—"you didn't."

George Bates ignored the open display of old wounds. He stared coldly into the policeman's face without flinching.

Detective Sergeant Xlong understood that his damaged features would fail to fill the foreigner with dread. Fine. He would come to know his man. Good. He could stretch. There would be time. George Bates might learn to appreciate the policeman's awkward early years of unending rain on the black mud of the police training field, the *chuff chuff chuff* of a portable electric generator slung in its wet leather harness over his exhausted shoulder, the copper teeth of the electrodes slick with the terror felt by those about to be questioned.

Would the foreigner be able to appreciate an adolescent policeman's awe at the unmistakably grudging nature of the prisoner's fear? Cupped, as it always was, within the hope that the roles would soon be reversed, the clothed stripped, and the tormentors in their turn tormented—it haunted him still.

Power was arbitrary: this was what kept the police from sleeping, what encouraged them to reproduce themselves, to hand down their myths and traditions, and to insist on certain fundamental enforcements.

"International conventions regulate entry procedures," Mr. Bates said stiffly.

"No doubt they do," Detective Sergeant Xlong agreed.

"No doubt they do." He picked up the passport and began chafing the gilt State Department eagle with his thumbnail. "But you are a man of wide experience. Surely you know more of such things than we do. I hope you don't think we're too stupid here."

The junior officer had begun digging at the bottom of a crate, tearing out handfuls of fruit and flinging them into the sea. It was not a pretty display. He badly wanted to participate.

"Perhaps I have a police brochure for you, one explaining in simple terms how to behave here—a list of quaint customs and regulations, with various violations and resultant quaint punishments. I'm sure you would find something like that useful."

Detective Sergeant Xlong made no move to produce such a pamphlet. Streaks of moisture slid down the walls like melting butter. The foreigner waited well. Good. Americans were said to be pragmatic. The detective sergeant felt the pleasure of a just man on the edge of an earned meal. He glanced down the shed. He would soon be required to attend to his junior officer.

George Bates repeated that he had simply come for his son. He wanted no unnecessary complications. Any difficulty could be cleared up. If there were fines to be paid, he would pay them.

The detective sergeant yawned self-consciously, wrenching open the top button on his police shirt. He mentioned that Mr. Bates should feel free to give a complete statement at this time. The offer was ignored. Detective Sergeant Xlong fumbled at his button with thick fingers, indicating his disappointment that the foreigner was not prepared to confide in him. Well, no matter. There was a shape to the process, as familiar to him as the slippery walls of his police office. He was hardly surprised. If the letters from the son had been drenched with poor emotional stability, those from the father had matched every watery excess with frozen shards of advice so perfunctory that the detective sergeant had passed each letter back to the servile little postman without comment. He even chose to ignore the abject manner in which that civil servant resealed the envelopes before placing them within the mossy folds of his gray rubber pouch. The policeman knew that the postman would later secretly peel off their stamps to mount on chips of bark in hopes of selling them to more than usually ignorant travelers.

"All right," said George Bates. "Where do I get this validation?"

"I am authorized to . . ."

"I assume there's a fee?"

The policeman nodded, lowering his eyes modestly to examine the blade of his thumbnail. He hoped Mr. Bates read the source of his display as embarrassment at the nature of the exchange. It would be useful to establish expectations.

"You'll take American dollars, won't you."

Was that a question? Detective Sergeant Xlong readjusted his cap. It never seemed quite right to him. He admitted he was prepared to accept foreign currency.

The policeman recalled seeing the son's melancholy face wandering around town, browsing through the row of souvenir shops that lined the road to the nearest ruins. The boy had the habits of a true tourist—perhaps, a junior officer had speculated, as camouflage. Why else would he have set so many souvenirs in motion? He mailed off everything he bought, some addressed to himself in care of places he had been, others forwarded to places he must have suspected he might be going; and at least once, the junior officer had concluded with a snort of triumph, he had knowingly dispatched some bauble toward a swamp no one would visit, not even a smuggler.

The detective sergeant had deflated his junior officer by pointing out that such a fact served to lessen the likelihood that the boy was trafficking illicitly. It was poor police work to unstring one's own case.

Detective Sergeant Xlong himself had never believed Philip was moving contraband. The crude figurines he bought, the mock daggers tricked out with chips of slag glass, the repetitive folk legends stitched in hasty appliqué—they rarely found the boy again, and the policeman knew he thought that just as well. Philip never wanted to own them. He didn't even need the momentary pleasure of their passing from another's hands into his own. He just liked to think of them out wandering through the postal lanes—flotsam orphaned on the waves of international regulations, plaintively seeking him.

Philip wrote to his father how occasionally a particularly tenacious souvenir would manage to track him down. Reintroduced into the equation by some garlicky and implacable Oriental concierge, it would confront him like a filial thug, whimpering at the injustice done it—a battered parcel bearing his own name louvered as a wound, that accusation alone unchanged among a series of progressively hopeless forwarding addresses.

The sight of such parcels' presumptive solidity inevitably caused a brief thud of self-consequence, and the bundle itself took on a karmic significance—although not to a degree that might tempt him to unwrap it.

Such behavior confused younger members of the police. Had Philip not at last become involved in a possibly criminal activity, Detective Sergeant Xlong might have contrived something for no other reason than to maintain decorum. He did not like messiness.

"How much is this going to cost me, anyway? Ten dollars? Twenty?"

❖❖❖❖❖❖❖❖❖❖❖

Children spotted him first. They came running up out of the water in twos and threes, stumbling awkwardly, unaccustomed to the dry sand. A few of the boys wore rags or frayed bits of rope knotted about their necks, but most were naked. They shouted like gulls chummed with fish chunks, some brandishing sharpened sticks, some waving fleshless arms above their heads, bits of clam shell gripped like choppers.

Older girls rose slowly from the shadows of strangler figs, bright skirts bound haphazardly beneath distended bellies, some pregnant, most only malnourished. They clutched each other and stared dumbfounded at George Bates.

He dropped his luggage in the sand and glanced about him. Help with the bags would obviously be welcomed, yet Detective Sergeant Xlong hesitated in the doorway of the customs shed.

The children ringed George Bates, dancing against each other, keeping a safe distance.

"Hello!" one shouted tentatively.

From the approaching steamer, the banks of the estuary beach would have appeared to end in a blank wall of jungle sloping up to misty blue mountains. Gaps in the vegetation could now be seen where dirt roads led off into the interior. Two hundred meters upriver from the customs dock, an ancient riverboat rotted against a second, smaller pier.

"Hello! Hey!" The children laughed. They grabbed an unwary boy and threw him at Mr. Bates. He scrambled past, his penis protected in a scaly fist. The tip of a stick pricked the back of Mr. Bates's knee. He turned, and a child from the front darted in to slap the outermost suitcase. Everyone cheered.

"Listen . . ." Mr. Bates began.

"You! Hey!" They laughed. "Hello!"

Mr. Bates reached into his pocket and produced a handful of coins. Two of the older boys tried to snatch the skirt off a girl in front of him. They grabbed her by the arms, extending their rubber tongues, while a third boy bent to pry at her ankles.

"Hello!"

Detective Sergeant Xlong kicked the circle apart, grunting with satisfaction as his boot scored against buttocks too slow to avoid it. He loosened his belt a notch, preparing to introduce himself, now friendly, apparently somewhat less self-conscious in his role. It was hot, wasn't it? He didn't think it was hot like this in the U.S.A. He himself had not been to Mr. Bates's fine country; although, if the opportunity should arise, he would be quick to take it.

"Your police . . ." he began, then turned to drive back the closing ring of children.

George Bates made his way to a taxi parked before the smaller pier. All four tires were flat, and the engine had been stolen. He stopped beside the crippled machine and fitted his fingers into the constellation of bullet holes in the front fender.

Detective Sergeant Xlong examined the stains on the sweatband of his police cap. He began whipping it in the air. The cap would immediately rot if he didn't keep after it. A bold child crept forward to touch Mr. Bates's arm; the policeman sent him sprawling.

"These children are very interested in you."

Mr. Bates ignored the comment. He coldly asked the policeman if he could get a porter to help with his bags.

"Only at the airport. Here we have nothing."

"There's an airport?"

"Yes. A very fine one. Unfortunately, there are no flights to it at present."

"Then why are the porters there?"

"They are optimists, Mr. Bates, as are all of us here in the Republic."

"You! Hey!"

The policeman joined George Bates for his trek up into the jungle. The mob of children trailed them from a safe distance. It would rain, the policeman observed. George Bates said nothing; he was clearly exhausted. It rained at least twice in the morning, the policeman continued. And of course the afternoons were no better.

Detective Sergeant Xlong wondered if Mr. Bates might not like to talk about his problems, confide the anguish felt by a troubled father far from home in bad weather. It was always off-season here. Visitors dwelt unduly on the climate. In fairness, it should be mentioned that during a brief dry period after the monsoon, an entire day could pass with no more than a single storm.

George Bates glanced at Detective Sergeant Xlong, who smiled and squared his cap. He realized he talked more than was usual for a policeman. It was the jungle coming through, insisting upon itself like the wet weight of leaves on one's face, the green mud sucking at one's ankles.

Mr. Bates was not to worry about his exhaustion. No one did well at the beginning. The air was too thick here, too stagnant. Detective Sergeant Xlong himself—born up-river from a mother partially submerged; scraped down with serrated leaves that left to this day comb-ridges on the unaired quarters of his groin; cured over a fire smoking from wood so green, so wet, so hopeless with fungus that it rarely achieved a proper burn; and suspended above the mud of his birth by cords that smelled of the insides of animals—even he became depressed by the weight of the jungle, by dread of the day's weather.

George Bates must no doubt be longing for a hotel. The Royal Prince was the finest in the area, and repairs were going forward as well as could be expected. He could perhaps calm himself with thoughts of a private bathroom, a gin and tonic, and a recent copy of the *Times*. Some food, perhaps? Perhaps a woman?

Mr. Bates might be interested in an explanation of the role of the police in this matter. The fundamental concept

here was cooperation. From this all benefits flowed. Mr.
Bates was not a young man; he tired easily. But perhaps
he had, on his long journey from America, discovered that
he was still self-reliant. This was the glory of the human
condition, was it not? Although Detective Sergeant Xlong,
in the course of his duties as an officer and defender of the
law, had himself been badly stabbed, shot, clubbed,
kicked, bombed, poisoned, and burned by his fellow
humans, he nevertheless retained a qualified enthusiasm
for the human condition.

Be that as it may, Mr. Bates might do well to realize
that there were definite limitations to his personal state of
self-reliance. He should regulate his activities accordingly.
Harmony—that was the great thing.

"I appreciate your advice, Detective Sergeant."

"Nothing. Part of my duty. As very few foreigners come
here, we of the police are always interested when someone arrives within our frontiers."

George Bates froze in his tracks. A black snake was
coiled in the path before him. He had been so distracted
by the suffocating pressure from the jungle that he'd almost walked directly onto it. One of the children jumped
forward with a shout and kicked it out of the way. Upon
closer inspection, Mr. Bates saw that it was nothing more
than a curved length of high-pressure hosing, burned at
each end.

"War trash," said the policeman. "As you may know, this
area has been troubled by political unrest. We are required to be very careful when dealing with possible
enemies."

The child who had kicked away the dead bit of hose

now made a great show of dancing out in front of George Bates, clearing the smallest twigs from his path in an exaggerated display of concern.

"Welcome to the Republic," the detective sergeant said as they paused on a slight hill overlooking the town.

"Why are all these children still following us?"

"Not us, Mr. Bates, you. It's you they like."

White tropical thunderheads collected above the mountains beyond the town. Mr. Bates followed the policeman across the open hillside, his feet no doubt awash in his socks. The earth was charred, but in places curved furrows had been opened, as if in preparation for a mass burial of pythons.

"Cassavas, Mr. Bates, if the farmers have not forgotten. There are no seasons here, so they plant any time; this makes them negligent."

"Cassavas?"

"Have you never seen those fleshy rootstocks eased from the soil? Starchy, agreed, but they can be fermented."

A child trapped a weasel. After expertly choking the terrified creature sufficiently to quiet it, he thrust it in front of Mr. Bates's face.

"The Royal Prince Hotel, you can see it from here, snug in its location behind the movie theater. Do you like *My Fair Lady*? The final reels have been with us for almost a year now."

The children bent with shouts of laughter, and even the policeman was pleased when the weasel gathered itself enough to begin hissing at Mr. Bates.

"It likes you."

George Bates leveled a slow stare at Detective Sergeant

Xlong. He was not amused. He turned to take advantage of the opportunity afforded by the clearing; he would familiarize himself with the town below.

The child yelled something in his native language.

"Do you want to pet this animal?" the policeman translated.

"Certainly not."

From the top of the hillside, it was a short walk to the mud terraces of poor huts which rimmed the town. Although these structures were little more than lattice walls thatched with rotting fronds, they could be seen as forming a bulwark against the encroachment of the jungle.

The child said something else.

"Would you care to eat it, then?"

George Bates turned abruptly to confront the policeman. He demanded to know the exact charges against his son.

Detective Sergeant Xlong scratched his ear. That was a very good question, and one for which they hoped to contrive an equally good response. At this point, a careful statement of the nature of the procedures commonly followed here in the Republic might be in order.

"What charges?" George Bates insisted.

The policeman explained he had every intention of placing his hand more directly into this matter of Mr. Bates's son. They could perhaps work together. Such results would be superior to anything either developed on his own. Had Mr. Bates never opened a tin of sardines? Was there not an efficiency to the arrangement of the heads? It was thus with the police. Pleasure was nurtured where order prevailed.

"What are you talking about?"

The detective sergeant nodded sheepishly. His English was not perfect. He apologized in advance for all mistakes.

George Bates continued to stare at him. He stated flatly that he was fully capable of deciding with whom, and when, and how to proceed. He again demanded to be informed of the charges against Philip.

"Conspiracy to commit." The policeman touched his fingertips together. "If not something firmer. Such writs here are as common as . . ."

"Conspiracy to commit what?"

"What indeed?" the policeman agreed. He was pleased that Mr. Bates could share their uncertainty. What indeed—the very question they had been asking themselves.

George Bates interrupted him. There was a man named Sprague. Who was he?

"Sprague?"

"You *do* know the name."

"He is not a person you would enjoy, Mr. Bates."

"No doubt. Nevertheless, my son has evidently become involved in some nonsense with him."

"Sprague has spread a trail of outrages the length of the Archipelago. The man is a common criminal. But this investigation hasn't yet . . ."

"What investigation?"

"I can appreciate your confusion, Mr. Bates. Quite frankly, things seldom happen here as neatly as we of the police could wish."

"If this Sprague is so bad, why haven't you arrested him?"

"We have, more than once. Charges brought against him fail to succeed for lack of proof. We of the police do our best to achieve convictions. We understand the value of evidence. My junior officers collect whatever is lying about, occasionally adding to our store with refuse from previous crimes—an indication, I'm afraid, that they haven't quite mastered the basic principles of . . ."

George Bates snatched up his bags and stalked off along the crest of the hill.

". . . due process."

The detective sergeant trailed after Mr. Bates, hoping the prospect of civilization below might improve the man's disposition. Mr. Bates was unfair. He should attempt to adjust. The members of the police were nothing other than a skin fitted over the society they attempted to protect. They thus retained the shape of any inequity, and were not to be blamed for flaws in the criminal justice system. Codes attached to a democratic republic that had been carved wholly out of jungle were bound to be clumsy. Regulating an organized state required a spirit of inventiveness, yet the rank and file of the police militia still half lingered in the morning swamps of childhood. They were amphibian here. This accounted for the green tinge to the skin, the fondness for drinking water scummed with algae.

And it was difficult to keep all the evidence together during the course of a trial. Anything of worth was soon stolen and sold on the black market. His junior officers were not to be condemned. Witnesses wandered away and were not seen again. Those they recovered forgot what was to be said. Searches were made for materials suitable for criminal prosecutions, but little was turned up: a belt buckle, a dead watch, a clutch of buttons or set of knuckle bones—such things were of slight influence in a court of law.

More children scrambled up to greet Mr. Bates as he pushed his way into the path that led through the upper mud banks. Detective Sergeant Xlong saw the curved hem of rain begin to sweep down, darkening the blue slopes of jungle beyond. He knew the foreigner would never make the hotel before the storm reached them. The mud in the middle of the downhill path was treacherous with morning sewage. Mr. Bates began picking his way along the upper rim, being careful not to trip over any of the smaller children who tumbled across his path.

"Mr. Bates," the policeman shouted toward his back. "Here you have no fear of the enemy guerrillas, understand?" He spread his arms apart to indicate a perimeter loosely including both the town and the surrounding flanks of jungle. "We of the police are vigilant and decisive!"

George Bates ignored him. Clouds rushed down over them, blotting out the sun and dragging in the first flat layers of rain. Detective Sergeant Xlong squared his cap and set off down the path. It was time to get wet.

◆《◆《◆《◆《◆《◆《◆《

Detective Sergeant Xlong sat up alone in the night gloom of his police office. George Bates would be asleep. He wondered what kind of dreams the old man had. For the policeman, all dreaming was a failure. An occasional sense that his insomnia had wandered momentarily beyond the rim of consciousness was the closest he was able to come. The few afterimages he recalled from these brief excursions were as faint as photographs glimpsed in a magazine being read by somebody else.

He liked George Bates. He was glad that the man had come. Sprague's involvement in the case guaranteed complications. There would be a great deal for Mr. Bates and him to accomplish.

Once he had assumed the foreigner was settled in his room, the detective sergeant had laboriously spelled out a message to him, explaining that further information indicated Philip might no longer be in town. He had sent this to the hotel, along with an invitation to dinner. Mr. Bates had not replied. The detective sergeant was disappointed, but he decided that silence simply meant the man was exhausted by his long journey.

Detective Sergeant Xlong removed his leather boots and placed them neatly on his desk. He rolled open the largest drawer. A wet mat of black ashes caked the bottom. He pinched out a small wad and began rubbing it into his boots.

He wondered if the old man still dreamed about women. Might he be in the habit of constructing night companions from the materials of casual daylight accidents? Detective Sergeant Xlong hoped so. Everyone needed something, no matter how ephemeral. An encounter with love, even if only the brief spasm shaking one in one's solitary bed, was not to be ignored. The policeman reminded himself that he alone was calm, hard, dark, sufficient. He applied more ashes, recalling how police flames curled the pages of impounded magazines, how the sophisticated dyes essential for the glossy flesh tones of female nudes burned green and blue, licking against the metal sides of his desk drawer—like most things, most interesting at the moment of change.

George Bates could help with the investigation. He could pin relationships to each other, perhaps even attach Sprague to his crimes. The more the policeman thought about it, the better it pleased him. Sprague was the key, he would explain in an official voice. Mr. Bates, of course, would reply that he had not come halfway around the world in order to entangle himself in local problems. Granted, the policeman would nod. Perfectly reasonable. Mr. Bates would then think he was off the hook. But, the policeman would say, capturing the man's attention and then pausing. But what? Mr. Bates would have to ask. The detective sergeant would at that point come up with something fine. He would remind the foreigner of their roles. He would couch his explanation so forcefully that Mr. Bates would become unable to forget who he was and what he could do about it.

The policeman removed a sock and began polishing the toes of his boots. He would explain to Mr. Bates that there was no cause for haste, and—he would conclude in a careful voice, perhaps underlined with a subtle and appropriate gesture—none for anger. He would add something reassuring about the brotherhood of man. Mr. Bates would have to recognize the value of a friend in the police.

He yawned. This was a good world. He was hard enough, he told himself, and calm. And he understood the pleasures to be found in the stillness of a photograph, as well as those to be drawn from its destruction. But now he was tired. He would have liked to edge into George Bates's dreams, to pluck up the flap of his sleep and insert a single patch of human skin pinched between thumb and fore-finger, the cuticles taut, the pink of the nail polish glowing in candlelight like the insides of freshly opened clams. He did like George Bates. He wanted to give him something. Would the old man still have a taste for romance?

The policeman removed his other sock. He considered the hands of his little friend, Moule. He could recommend her to George Bates. Her powerful fingers alone had the ability to drain him from himself. He opened his shirt and ran the sock under his arms and across his chest. A police-man kept himself clean and neat. Hygiene was essential. "Moule," he said aloud. She was a masseuse who had learned her trade in Hong Kong. It was said that few understood the human body as well as those who learned their trade there.

Detective Sergeant Xlong stood up and stretched. He was tired. He looked at his boots. They were ready for tomorrow. Boots, he thought with pleasure, my boots. Did he have a fresh shirt? He would have to check.

"You are under arrest," he said aloud, and crammed his socks into his pocket. What a wonderful world.

He strolled across the exercise yard to his quarters. George Bates might be dreaming of him at that very moment. What would his face look like, wrapped inside the foreigner's sleep? He thought it would look good.

The rain began again. He did not hurry. A policeman was not hurried by the weather. It was natural for George

Bates to wonder what his son had done. Detective Sergeant Xlong assumed that it would be up to him to produce a likely hypothesis once the father had adjusted himself to the altered rhythms here.

He tested his police hammock. Sections were rotten, but it would carry him another night. He hoped George Bates had pulled the blankets up around his ears. The night rain might awaken him. He probably hadn't closed his windows. His bed would become wet; the floor would be slick with rain. He might catch a chill. The detective sergeant made a mental note to say something firm to the hotel staff first thing in the morning.

He closed his eyes. He tried to shift himself toward sleep. It was the duty of the police to anticipate and appreciate the motives of others without allowing them to impede the flow of an investigation.

Nothing—a comforting thought, but he was still wide awake.

He relaxed his toes, relaxed his ankles, and checked to see if he could jump directly to his stomach. No luck. It was knotted. Should he go to Moule? She would be snug in her little bed, her little liqueur bottle on the floor beside her. What was she wearing? Rainbow nets?

Tonight he would not see her. He began again at his knees.

Tell me, Mr. Bates, he would say tomorrow. Why was your son so unhappy? Well, Detective Sergeant, the foreigner would reply, the boy has been troubled since childhood.

Nice, he thought, and kneaded his thighs. They would

be two men, two fathers, although of course his progeny had as yet not extended beyond a group of completed police sequences—the offspring of his fist.

They would talk. They would discuss why Philip had never wanted to be anything. Mr. Bates might ask advice. The policeman would consider the question. Philip had wondered what to study in college and his father had evidently spent hours on the subject, finally presenting a number of courses, each designed to hold open as many options as possible. Philip had agreed to the first and followed it. At graduation, his name had been misspelled on his diploma. Mr. Bates would explain to the policeman how he had wondered why Philip hadn't corrected the error. Didn't the school have them check such things before they printed them? The detective sergeant would nod agreeably. And what did your son reply? That he had checked it. Well, well. And hadn't noticed? Had noticed, Mr. Bates would then say in a troubled voice. Well, well, the policeman would repeat sympathetically. Well, well.

He swung out of his hammock. He was too excited. He began to try to loosen his legs with calisthenics. The construction of appropriate historical probabilities was one of the fundamental pleasures of the police. Once established, the ground for action then produced its own inner tempo. Soft and hard, in and out—the members of the police simply followed.

He dipped and straightened, dipped and straightened. He had power. His thighs were like bricks packed in sacks of grease. He inhaled, held it, exhaled. In and out, off and on—he glanced at his hammock. Should he try to sleep again? He dipped and straightened.

C. K. SPRAGUE IS INVOLVED

"I'm Sprague."

George Bates looked up.

"They say how you been asking about me. Well, like I say, I'm Sprague, C. K. Sprague."

George Bates nodded. On the bar before him was a creased photograph of his son. Each time he unfolded it, the white line of damage across the middle grew slightly wider. Philip's face would soon be distorted beyond recognition.

Detective Sergeant Xlong in his police office listened patiently to his junior officer's report. Mr. Bates's retreat to the basement bar beneath the Royal Prince came as no surprise. It had been a fruitless day. At the end, some minor civil servant pawing through moldy documents had apparently suggested a course of action identical in every step to the one Mr. Bates had been following, but

25

in the reverse order. Bureaucratic insensitivity has driven stronger men than George Bates underground.

The junior officer lingered beside a glass showcase containing the police collection of blunt instruments. Detective Sergeant Xlong ignored the fresh leather trim he had sewn to his police shirt. He knew his young officer wanted to rush back and insert himself into the conspiracy, but he simply smiled and nodded and signed another warrant. The detective sergeant intended to occupy himself with minor duties. He could wait; he trusted his intuition.

"Stroke," said C. K. Sprague, dragging his left leg. "Damn doctor had to be paid cash. 'C. K.,' he said, 'little sac of blood exploded inside your brain box.' He told me I might never be beyond my bed again." Sprague turned to show that his left arm was also partially frozen. "There were days when I believed him. Those first times out, going down the street, even the damn dogs weren't afraid of me. Nothing worse than that. But I'm not killed, not yet." A twisted smile tugged at the slack meat on the left side of his face. "Although you can bet there are those who'd be glad to see me dead!"

He hauled himself up onto the barstool, loosening his stiff leg with the butt of his fist. He asked if Mr. Bates had been informed of the disastrous state of local tin production. Sprague considered himself one of the original victims. He had been cleaned out years ago, his role as managing partner stolen from him by a rogue geologist.

The bartender waited for a word from Mr. Bates; he still hadn't said anything. Sprague's tongue cleared his lips. George Bates asked if he could buy him a drink.

"Well, I guess just one more wouldn't hurt. Nature's most perfect food, like they say; just a meal in a glass.

"You probably want to know if I'm one of those fellows that wallows in the past. Not me! The future's what I, what I wallow, unh, look forward to. Hell, you think I don't know how bad everything's been? I could tell you stories about upriver, guys cutting each other up—but bitter? Not me. I could tell you how that damn geologist traded his bride's dowry for a ton and a half of commercial TNT and blew the more useless members of his new family directly into the twentieth century. I was there. C. K. Sprague was present and accounted for. That geologist held up a stick of dynamite. 'So much for the Stone Age,' he said, and lit the fuse. He explained how what he was doing was accelerating evolution, but what he wanted was fellows who'd go down into wet mines. You ever been in a tropical mine, Mr. Bates? No? I wouldn't think so. No place for a person to be.

"But the past? To hell with it, you know? Here's to the future!"

George Bates mentioned that his son had written about a trip into the interior.

"The tin production business is sure not what it used to be," Sprague said, growing vague as his glass emptied. George Bates signaled toward the bartender.

The policeman divided his warrants into two piles. He was as at home with Sprague as with the curve of his own fist. "This warrant," he said to his junior officer, "is for you." The young policeman's face lit with pleasure. "Read it first," Detective Sergeant Xlong cautioned. "It's not what you think."

George Bates told Sprague that he knew his son was in trouble; although where he was and what the charges were against him remained unclear.

"Yeah, well, that's true. They do a poor job with their crimes around here. I speak from experience. But nobody made him go, you understand. He went of his own free will, like they say. He even made a point of saying that it was his choice, and he'd be the one to make it."

Sprague told how he was harassed by the police. They were afraid of his life-style. They saw him as a threat because he was free. Over the years, he had adopted the garb of the counterculture, just to let everybody know. The cops here charged him with vagrancy because they couldn't get a conviction for anything better. It was police brutality, pure and simple. He was used to it, though, on account of how he'd been free a long time—years, he said, years, and lucky to survive them, freedom here not being quite what it was in a country with adequate social services.

"I don't suppose you've ever been picked up for vagrancy?"

George Bates shook his head. He wondered if Sprague knew where he could find his son.

"Nothing's simple here," Sprague said. Mr. Bates had to understand that things took time because nobody was in much of a hurry. "You get used to it."

Sprague's troubles with the police had a long history. There was a time when he had been more of a match for them. They had probably assumed he was running dope, but his true career was in fighting cocks.

The police used to charge him with theft. He'd always

deny everything. Even when detained behind the wreck of some abandoned shed, feathers stuck to his whiskers with coins of dried blood, he'd reply with such righteous indignation that younger members of the force were filled with doubt and had to be taken aside and reassured.

He didn't know anything about any stolen birds, Sprague would insist; and when the single scaly claw protruding from beneath his boot was called to his attention, no one could have been more surprised than he was. He'd never seen the bird before. He didn't know how it got there. Sheer happenstance, no doubt.

A witness might then be provided to help Sprague recall the evidence in question. It was a fighting cock, a loser. Yes, as a matter of fact, he did remember, now that they mentioned it. But the cock had been paid for. Didn't the boy show up with the money? Why, that little thief! Sprague vowed to skin him alive, paddle his bottom, dust his britches!

Sprague had no difficulties with remorse. The police might have gradually wearied of his problems had it not been for the fact that, not only were the birds frequently unpaid for, Sprague was in the habit of thinning his stable through decapitation, executing feckless competitors with a single snap of his teeth—a bit of machismo that, despite their comparative lack of sophistication, the citizens of the Republic found disgusting.

The police received constant complaints. Shrill voices outside their windows insisted that the foreigner's crime was repulsive. Children should be protected from such sights. Angry mothers organized themselves. The members of the police turned to Detective Sergeant Xlong for leadership. He had no choice but to prepare warrants.

"We adapt," Sprague said. "We learn new tricks in new situations. That's how come we Americans survive so good."

His method of executing unwanted birds was necessary since it showed everybody where his head was—evidently the single most important activity in his life. He had been misunderstood. He wanted what was fair. He wasn't bitter, just determined to let everybody know they couldn't push C. K. Sprague around anymore. He was free.

Sprague explained that successful performance could be ascribed to determination, proper timing, and a resilient stomach. George Bates asked why the same effect couldn't be achieved by simply wringing the bird's neck.

"Shock value loosens the fingers," Sprague replied. "It opens the pockets." He only wanted what was fair, but sometimes you had to bend things in order to get it. He also thought it was a little undignified to wring a bird's neck in the cockpit. All that twisting and waiting and twisting and waiting—you could lose your momentum. Dignity was as important as freedom.

"Just like that bullfighting they got, you know? You got your crowd and your animal and your moment of truth. Same here. But in cockfighting, if you scrape up a few vegetables you also got a pretty good curry." Sprague admitted the meat might be a little stringy, but the flavor was unique; "right out of the jungle," he said approvingly, "real natural."

The policeman stood and stretched and closed his files. He had the evening's tasks to distribute. He looked in the squad room, but none of his men were there. Should he check the police pantry? They often huddled behind the butcher's table, picking at the storeroom lock, intent on stealing food. Why were they always so hungry? He returned to his desk to wait. He'd give them another ten minutes, then fire a shot out the window. The sound of live ammunition would bring them running.

Detective Sergeant Xlong removed his police cap to test for fresh patches of rot. His mind momentarily drifted to thoughts of his little friend Moule. He wondered what she was wearing.

"Have you had a taste of our local whiskey yet, Mr. Bates? No? Then C. K. Sprague insists you allow him to do the honors. No! Not a word! Don't thank me. We're just like this family here, you and me and him," he said, gesturing toward the bartender. "It's the least I can do for the father of the fellow who went so out of his way on my behalf. The boy's a damn dynamo, that's what he is!"

"Philip?"

"Well, maybe not so much a dynamo, no, but you could tell he has promise. Hell, promise, boy, he's got more promise than anything else—no offense, Mr. Bates, nothing personal. And he's loyal, too, although he does tend to moon around some, come and go some. But promise? Take it from me, I've never seen anybody with so much of that out in front of him.

"He'd get going on one thing or another, never really deciding, you know, just wondering what he ought to do. 'What do you *want* to do?' I'd ask him, and his face'd get all splotchy the way it does, you know, like a fellow who just swallowed a fly. He'd say he didn't want to do any-

31

thing. He'd say people'd always be telling him he could be anything he wanted. The trouble was, he'd have to be the one to do the wanting. He said he was keeping his eye open for that, just being on the lookout for whatever it was he was going to be wanting so that when it showed up, he'd be ready for it. When you come to think about it, the boy has a lot of freedom. It just doesn't seem to do him much good.

"But I'll tell you one thing, and you can bank on this— C. K. Sprague's as good as his word, better sometimes, as a matter of fact—what the boy's got is a future, most of which he hasn't used yet."

The bartender appeared with two cocktails.

"The local whiskey," Sprague said, patting over his pockets.

"Eight thousand *lolls.*"

"That's funny," said Sprague, twisting to try to touch his left rear pants pocket with his good hand and almost falling off the barstool with the effort. "I must've forgotten my wallet. You want to just put this on my bill?"

The bartender repeated the numbers.

"Establishing credit is hard here, Mr. Bates, particularly for an individual such as myself without ready references. I try to explain to them how in America the whole point of a successful business is to try to get you to buy something you don't need and can't pay for, but they don't seem to catch on. 'Revolving credit plans,' I tell them, speaking from experience. 'You get on and you go around and around and around. Pretty soon the whole house belongs to the fellow that installed the shower curtain.' You'd think they'd see how it works, but they don't.

Cash is what they want. No way to get a repeat customer coming back if every time you sell something you ask him to pay for it. No business sense here, which is why I've had such a hell of a time with that smeltery of mine. I'll tell you, Mr. Bates. Sometimes it seems like I don't get but about half of what I paid for and not much more of what I didn't. I mean in value, you understand. It's hard to make a profit here."

George Bates counted out eight 1,000-*loll* notes. He no doubt knew that would make a sufficient reply.

"Thanks, Mr. Bates, but don't forget, this one's on me. Right this very moment I'm figuring plans on how to pay you back. C. K. Sprague knows a debt when he sees one."

George Bates needed information. He would be willing to work for it, and Sprague was obviously the place to begin.

Detective Sergeant Xlong had begun to distribute his warrants. In the intervals between the appearances of his men, he had scraped his boots and gone over every inch of his police cap. Once more mildew had been defeated. The inside of his leather belt was a particularly troublesome area, requiring every bit of his expertise. He might have abandoned it were it not for the row of cartridges snugly seated in their wet loops.

He took out his hand mirror, conscious of the moist heat in the constricted sections of his trousers. He was a man. His shoulders began to cramp as he examined his face, carefully scraping a patch of gray from the lobe of his ear. Again he considered visiting his little friend. Moule might be settled behind her screen, cooling herself with a silk fan. Her eyes would be on the street, and her little white teeth would show behind her parted lips as she awaited a change in the weather.

Love, he thought, but his mind still lingered on the subject of fungus.

The policeman knew George Bates would have begun to bend Sprague toward what he wanted. Perhaps he simply delayed a round or two, the intention obvious in the wad of cash uncoiling on the bar. Sprague would talk. He would tell how Philip had gone upriver on a mission of reconnaissance. Sprague had heard a rumor that the rogue geologist's health was failing. He had not been able to go along with Philip, he would claim, because of his own disabled condition.

Two of the youngest officers stumbled in, self-consciously trying to hide the food they had stolen. He put his arms around their shoulders in an avuncular manner. They reminded him of himself when he was young. He smiled at how he would form their careers; and as he did so, he perceived the first faint strains of "Moon River" coming from his little friend's phonograph. Moule was lonely. Had she loosened her bodice to encourage air circulation? The policeman selected a warrant. He told the two young officers what to do and sent them on their way.

Perhaps it appeared unlikely to Mr. Bates that Sprague had any legal claim to the tin smeltery. Nevertheless, the man would insist he had believed his chance for justice had arrived. Why Philip had agreed to the adventure was unclear to the policeman. The boy's father, however, might be somewhat less surprised by it. And he would not accept Sprague's promise to repay Philip as the reason for the trip—Philip had plenty of money available. Sprague would try to explain why he hadn't done anything when Philip failed to return. Messages had been sent from upriver suggesting matters were under control; but there was never any specific information about the geologist, the one thing that Sprague had most wanted.

Sprague's brief flurry of activity when word reached him that Philip was in danger of detention did not confuse the police. They knew he would not dare to go upriver alone.

Moo-oon Ri-ver, lah, la-la-la-lahhh . . .

"Why would he be in preventive custody? Preventing him from doing what?"

"Hard to say, Mr. Bates. Upriver things get out of hand right away. You can blame it on that damn geologist. That fellow's got no sense of how to get along. Overeducated, that's what I say. You get to where you know so much you can't make do with the simple pleasures anymore. He cracked, that's all; and we're still cleaning up the mess.

"I guess you think we don't do so good here with our business associates. But you know, Mr. Bates, that Philip seemed to have an idea all his own about what he was going to do up there. I used to wonder about that. What if he was planning to grab it all for himself? No offense, Mr. Bates, like I said, business here's not as neat as it is back there in Los Angeles. What we got here is a jungle economy, real elemental and straight out of the river. Natural, like I said. Boy! Is it natural! Sometimes it's enough to make you wonder if nature's all it's cracked up to be."

George Bates wanted to know why there would be a problem in going directly upriver. He'd been told the river packet no longer ran on a regular schedule. Was that really because of guerrilla activity?

"Well, yeah," said Sprague, his good hand prying apart the wings of his nostrils to aid his breathing. "There's still a lot of that around the Archipelago, although the rebels they got here are nothing like the ones they got over where they got real wars. Hell, here the fighting's no better than the telephones.

"It's sagged, Mr. Bates. A lot of the rebels have lost their enthusiasm. The younger ones complain how they've been sold out, but I guess that's true everywhere now. Not much chance for advancement. Most of the participants at the top are related, so all you get is a bunch of family members taking turns cutting up each other's scrubs. No chance for growth there. A few years ago, it was a proper four-footed conflict, mostly thanks to that geologist. He never understood the basic principles of management. He'd fumble around, trying to pack together some program that would make use of the bit of human potential we were able to get our hands on. I'd just about begin to be feeling hopeful about the whole thing when he'd say there was something we were forgetting. 'What?' I'd say, knowing I wasn't going to like it much. 'Verifiability,' he'd say with a grin, but I knew what he meant was dynamite.

"Just not practical, you know?

"Once enough people got mad at him, a TV crew from the BBC showed up, and that was the beginning of the end. Television, I'll tell you, Mr. Bates, it's like ants; it gets into everything. As soon as those rebels heard about the cameras, they knew they'd have to do something to earn a few minutes of prime time. There's nothing like being taken seriously for making a fellow squirm—particularly if he's of an ideological persuasion, like they say, and dependent on foreign funding.

"The rebels set charges and blew up the hotel. The police caught a few of the squad and put them against the nearest wall. After that, the struggle collapsed into a stalemate. The BBC let it be known that if nothing else was going to happen, they were pulling out. With the hotel gone, there was no place for them to exercise their expense accounts. They gave the rebels a week to work up something good; the rebels couldn't do it. There're still a few hotheads shooting up the jungle, but for the most part, they're back to hanging around the smeltery, trying to keep their feet dry.

"You can see I'm cynical, Mr. Bates. C. K. Sprague admits he's cynical when it comes to the promise of group activity. The rebels stay in their part and the police stay in theirs, and if nobody wanders out too far nobody gets hurt.

"Of course, you've got to have your jungle to make a situation like that work. That's why they're back at that smeltery. It's more or less neutral turf, by which we mean swamps so miserable nobody wants them. Whatever happens is half underwater. That's why it can be hard to figure out who's doing what to whom, as they say.

"C. K. Sprague is not hopeful about this arrangement. Nothing ever gets settled. That's what causes the commercial community to just sit around and suck on its tongue. Hell, when I was first on the river, we'd've gone up there with rifles and shot up the bushes some. That would've solved it.

"Which is one thing that old rogue geologist has—a good feeling for weapons, I mean. He's a natural. I've seen that fellow with his butt in the mud, cradling an assault rifle like it was a newborn baby and humming one of those lullabies under his breath.

"Nuts is what he is, the only fellow I ever saw that took pleasure in talking to a piece of equipment.

"Your scientists, Mr. Bates, I'll tell you, when they go, look out! He had this old cannon mounted on the nose of his lead barge. He'd stuff it with all kinds of junk—scrap metal and broken glass; he'd chop up old barbed wire and put that in, even sharp bits of rock, 'anything that'd make a hole,' he used to say. And then when somebody'd get too close to his tin, he'd let it off. It made a hell of a noise, and everything in front of it got scattered around.

"Sometimes I'm sorry we don't see eye to eye anymore, although of course he's the one that cost me my best fighting cock. He used to work for some oil company, one of those with a tricky name that doesn't really mean anything. He's done *them* some bad tricks, too, he and his wife. Stay out of her way, Mr. Bates. She's a match for her husband. She used to work those reverberating furnaces single-handed. She was a big woman, Mr. Bates, big everywhere. She was broad and deep, and she was always angry. You'd think she was mad at the ore itself, the way she burned the tin out of it. She'd clang home that ladle release lever so hard even the monkeys shut up.

"She took no pleasure in her work, Mr. Bates, and once

the tin was out into raw lumps and ready to be sold, she'd never give it a second look. It was the fire for her. I never saw anybody work as hard as she did. When the furnace is firing, you can't let it cool, so you got to be up two or three days and nights stoking, keeping the temperature just right. You can tell by the color of the eye of the fire. Nobody was as good at it as she was, and nobody got a chance to learn. It was all hers. Two or three days she'd be burning, her body swelling in the heat and cooking until she couldn't take any more and then she'd drop off her gloves and goggles and protective gear. She'd stagger down to the wet mud of the riverbank and sink down into the edge of the green water.

"She was a big woman, like I said, and when she walked past, everybody'd let up on what he was doing and just watch. We never could figure out her anger. Nobody'd say a word and nobody'd follow her. But every man had a feeling in himself for those times when she was down on the edge of the water, her clothes all soaked and sticking to her as she rubbed into the mud, trying to clear herself of the fire.

"I'll tell you, Mr. Bates, not a man there didn't have a thought about . . ."

Sprague turned suddenly and drained his glass. Two policemen had descended into the bar. One of them was the junior officer who had tried to harass Mr. Bates in the customs shed. Sprague pushed off the barstool, nearly fell, then hobbled toward the darkened rear section of the bar, working his way between piles of damaged furniture. He disappeared through a narrow opening behind a shattered billiards table tilted up against the back wall.

The pair of policemen stepped forward and demanded to see Mr. Bates's passport. He tossed it on the counter. The officer from the customs shed picked up the document and pretended to study it. He turned to ask something, evidently uncertain what to do. "This visa . . ." he began, then faltered. Mr. Bates looked at him steadily. He again conferred with his partner. After a brief debate, he returned the passport and departed, marching up the stairs obviously chagrined.

Detective Sergeant Xlong, about to set out, was delayed by one of his men, who rushed in, his arms full of old bones. He attended to the eager young officer gently but firmly. These were not human, he told him. "Buffalo," he said in the officer's own dialect, "water buffalo."

The young soldier hung his head as he rewrapped his find. Detective Sergeant Xlong knew he had only wanted to please, but it was essential that senior officers insist upon maintaining minimum standards for the quality of evidence.

❖((❖((❖((❖((❖((❖((❖((

"What? Wallow in the past? You wouldn't say that if you'd seen her when she was younger. Nobody could figure out what she got from that damn rogue geologist; but we'd watch her rub up against him, her face as smooth as butter."

George Bates peered out over the edge of the stacks of green bamboo. He said he was sure no one had followed him. Hiding here was silly.

"A couple minutes more can't hurt. Not that I care

about those cops, mind you. I just wasn't in the mood.

"Sometimes that fellow would go on down when she was cooling herself at the water's edge. He'd squat on the riverbank and tell her what he liked, which as near as we could figure was mostly batholiths and bedrock. We'd be stuck up on the hill with nothing but a rock crusher for company, and he'd be down there with that big, natural woman, going on about torsion joints in lava sheets. I mean, you got to understand, he'd just about on his own finished off her whole clan, and even so, he was the only man she ever wanted.

"You should've seen her, Mr. Bates. She was the biggest, strongest, most natural woman I ever saw. And that fellow wooed her with earth science, and it worked. Women, damn! If it hadn't been for the cockpits, I probably never would have had *any* pleasure in my life!"

Sprague led George Bates through a series of narrow alleys, always being careful to avoid the main streets. Mr. Bates said he wanted to return to his hotel, but Sprague insisted he had something important to show him.

"I had a hell of a cock once, a jungle red, the counter-punching king of the Archipelago. He was different, you know, a step above your common cock. He wouldn't eat anything but live meat, preferred baby mice. Many's the time I was crawling around on my hands and knees that I thanked my lucky stars I wasn't living in some fancy mansion where a fellow couldn't find one of those pink little squealers for when his cock wanted a bite!

"Not that way, Mr. Bates, straight down that road is the police barracks, although I guess you said you been there already.

"I'll tell you, Mr. Bates, I was a cowboy! Damn, but that cock and I had some good times! I called him the Pearl of the Monsoon Season on account of his preference for a wet pit, which is mostly what we got here. He was a natural mudder. He could stay light. His feathers didn't seem to load up with water like your average cock. There was something about a good typhoon that filled him with energy. His ruff'd rise up whenever a real ripper of a storm was coming. He loved to see the wind tearing shanties apart. I'd lash him to the roof so he could watch the sea smash boats and dump them up on the beach. The rain would slash at him, stringing out his wings and bending his feathers back the wrong way until they'd almost pull out. He'd just lean with it and hang on. Every time a tree would go over or somebody's roof would get flipped up and blown away, he'd call out a victory crow.

"He loved the weather when it was mean. But when it was hot and the rain was just coming straight down, his eyes'd get dull and he wouldn't take much pleasure in what was happening around him.

"The Pearl of the Monsoon Season was the only cock I ever fought that never once tried to fly. He was a walker. Hell, he held his head up. Hard and red, man. Sometimes I'd get the feeling he was trying to be something other than what he was, something *higher*, you know? Like he was hoping to evolve all on his own. I tried to tell him to be satisfied with what he'd accomplished. I tried to tell him how he was the greatest fighting cock this side of the Indian Ocean.

"I like to think he understood. You know?"

They passed down an alley so narrow they had to walk

single file. Sprague halted at a wooden door fitted directly into a blank mud wall. He opened it a crack, listened, then slipped quickly inside. George Bates followed him into a dark arena, one corner of which was filled with battered cock baskets. The walls and ceiling were wet and heavy with mold.

"Like being inside a turtle," said Sprague. Mr. Bates didn't answer. The odor of mildew was overpowering.

"This is where we used to fight, but now it's all moved upriver. That's where the real action is now. They made cockfighting illegal after the last terrorist bombing. I guess the government figured they'd make everything they could think of against the law so that if they wanted to detain somebody, they'd have something handy to quote."

"Do you think that's what happened to Philip?"

"Hard to say, Mr. Bates. But you got more crimes here than you got flies; and like you were saying about the market square, there's no shortage of flies."

George Bates said the stench of the abandoned cockpit was making him nauseated. He returned to the alley. Sprague paused in the doorway and looked back.

"A lot of good birds died in that room, Mr. Bates. It's like it's holy."

Sprague led Mr. Bates out toward the edge of town, still talking about the Pearl of the Monsoon Season. His main bird had come to so dominate the arena that it was hard to get fights. Even when the Pearl didn't kill the other bird, he would demoralize it so thoroughly that it couldn't do anything other than lie on its side with its eyes glazed, staring at the rain.

"When the Pearl got done with you, you weren't much more than a meal."

The cockpit had settled into a series of listless bouts, since anybody who won too many wouldn't have an excuse not to fight the Pearl. It was during this stalemate that the rogue geologist came to town for the first time, leading a bedraggled Malayan fighting gray on the end of a bit of hemp rope. "The man didn't even know enough to use a carrying basket," Sprague said in a hollow voice. "And that damn bird didn't have any more fighting spirit than a worn-out string mop."

Sprague had heard how the head scientist had abandoned a geological survey team and struck out on his own in the upriver jungles, but he'd never met him. He said he stepped up and introduced himself politely, the way you do when you're both foreigners, and mentioned that he had a fighting cock, too. The rogue geologist just smiled and never said a word—although there was a lot of nudging going on in the gallery, and a lot of reaching into pockets.

The fight was set. Every *loll* in town was riding on the Pearl. The geologist managed to cover each bet himself. Nobody had any doubts as to the outcome.

The two foreigners stepped into the center of the ring to heat up their birds. Sprague made a few comic remarks about the geologist's mother. "Your usual improbable stuff. You know. Just to loosen him up a little." Nothing happened, although the earth scientist's face drained from brick red to a sickly shade of beige.

Once the opening comments were finished, the two men held up their birds and went through the ritual of licking the gaffs—a customary demonstration that the tips were clean. "I'll tell you, Mr. Bates, the gleam in that fellow's eye as he sucked on those steel blades was disgusting. It's like he was tasting them."

The Pearl blew out in a flurry of golden feathers. The Malayan bird just stood stupidly in the mud. The Pearl cut left, then spurred back right, one wing out for balance but the other still tucked up as if the fight was hardly worth the effort.

"It was poetry, sheer poetry, the way he ventilated that fighting gray. I'll never be as good again as I was at that moment. You know what I mean?"

George Bates nodded. They were passing beside a grove of trees which had been hung with limp strips of white paper. The night sky had closed over with clouds. The jungle became even heavier in the darkness, obscuring the route back to the hotel.

Sprague admitted that the Malayan bird did have spunk. In spite of his wounds, he finally began fighting back, coming in high with his head up and wings out, trying to spur down from the top. This was just the kind of attack the Pearl of the Monsoon Season had been beating in every cockpit the length of the Archipelago. His technique was so simple he liked to add little flourishes occasionally, pretending to be in trouble in order to play to the crowd. He'd keep dodging to the same side, turning the other bird through tighter and tighter circles until it couldn't follow the angles any longer and landed off balance, its back exposed for the kill.

Sprague never had a doubt that he would win. Then he realized something was wrong. The Pearl seemed tentative. He had been playing his wounded bird routine and the fighting gray had pricked him a couple of times in passing. Nothing to worry about, Sprague had thought; but now he could tell that the Pearl was truly in trouble. His timing was off and his wing tips had a pathetic quiver Sprague had never seen.

He was about to jump into the ring and try to stop the fight when the geologist's gray drove a point right through the Pearl's brain, slamming the poor bird beak first into the mud.

"He didn't suffer. I guess I should be grateful for that. He was killed instantly.

"I'll tell you, Mr. Bates, that was the only time in my life that my eyes shed real tears. Not even when I heard that my cousin Ralph had been carried off by those driver ants they got in Africa had I felt so morose. I loved the Pearl. From the day of his death, I was going downhill. I lost my pleasure in life—a terrible thing, Mr. Bates, terrible."

Sprague told how the crowd had sat in stunned silence while the scientist filled his pockets with cash. He now owned most of the town. It was a sporting catastrophe. He finally had to resort to an ore sample sack to carry all the money.

Sprague knelt over the body of his fallen Pearl. He caught the sweet scent of poison from two meters away and knew he'd been had from the start. The geologist must have held a mouthful of poison—probably sap from the dumbcane vine. Fatal for a bird, it would only locally paralyze something as big as a man. The geologist couldn't have spoken if he'd wanted to.

Sprague snatched up the Malayan gray in both hands. He stuck the gray's head in his mouth and bit down hard. Nobody moved. He could feel spasms shake down the body of the dying bird as its blood pumped out onto his chest.

He stepped across the ring. The geologist knew what Sprague had done. He stood frozen. His ore sample sack hung down between his legs, swollen with victory. Sprague stopped before him, then spit the head out like a shot, right in his face.

"Well, Mr. Bates, we did some business a few months later and had a few laughs. We sort of formed an unofficial partnership. Without me, there never would have been a tin smeltery upriver. That fellow was good at finding things, but he had no mind for politics. It was dynamite or nothing. You can't run a business like that. You got to have some sense of continuity. I had to show him how to establish a working relationship with the members of the local labor force—those that were left, that is.

"Sometimes I thought I liked that fellow, but I didn't figure he'd be ready to rob me again.

"And you know, he never mentioned that cockfight once. It was always there like something unfinished between us. I kept waiting for him to bring it out into the open, but he never did.

"That geologist used to say how he'd come back from taking a load of tin down and see his old lady on the river-bank waiting for him, her face thickened from the heat and her black hair long and glossy in the sunlight, and two hundred years' history of the scientific method would fall away like shed skin. That's what he'd say he was

47

shucking, two hundred years of science. He said shale used to mean oil to him, but now it was just a word he'd whisper in her ear because she liked the sound of it."

Sprague stopped before a depression at the edge of the jungle. He cleared away some weeds and showed Mr. Bates a square stone half buried in the black loam. THE PEARL OF THE MONSOON SEASON had been scratched crudely on the surface. Sprague tried to kneel beside the grave, but his stiff leg refused to bend.

"I buried the Pearl," he said sentimentally. "I couldn't think of him as being just another curry.

"That damn geologist never said he was sorry about the Pearl. I thought maybe he'd come to depend on me more after he and his old lady broke up. She was from the same family that head cop is from—a bad bunch, all of them. They used to run this river, but now they're on hard times, just like the rest of us. When the geologist broke up with her, I thought we'd be able to work together again as a team, but he was too mean, too rotten inside, and when at last I had my back to the wall, like you say, and told him how the Pearl's death had been eating on me, he didn't understand. He'd completely forgotten.

"So, Mr. Bates, that geologist is the fellow your boy took on. If there's a crime, you can bet he's in on it. Once your scientist sours, he's a goner.

"But there may not be any crime. It may just all be family trouble."

Sprague moved away from the grave and turned back toward the path to town. The sky cover had thickened. Rain was only a few minutes away.

"Trouble? I've had my share, I'll tell you. But I guess

all the pain is worth it when I think about the times I saw my sweet Pearl perched on top of his carrying basket, head up, wings out—all feet and beak and bravery, yelling across the market square how he could tear apart any bird stupid enough to try him, and knowing, Mr. Bates, *knowing* he could do it!

"Sometimes I get down. Sometimes I can't get myself to sleep, I'm wishing so much I could be back there with him again. I was some cowboy, some puncher. You know how it is when you can't get to sleep?

"The death of the Pearl is the only thing I can't forgive, Mr. Bates. I owe that geologist one.

"But like I say, you get anything else you want, you just let me know. C. K. Sprague is available and getting more so. Maybe I was better than I'm ever going to be, but damn if I don't have a few teeth left in my head yet. So, wallow? To hell with it. I'm a scrapper!"

❖❖❖❖❖❖❖❖❖❖❖❖❖

"An underfed coroner, Mr. Bates, has spoiled more than one investigation. His nasal voice whines through the tin hole of the telephone, wheedling chemicals, peevish because of the rejected demand for disposable blades. I have seen his face when he is sulking in his stripping shed. His squinty eyes are the color of old eggs; he seldom shaves, for he knows no one will invite him to lunch. Official requests are ignored; backlogs soon pile up. Thick plastic envelopes partially filled with unclean liquids are discovered in suggestive places, and maintenance costs alone eat up the budget of the police.

"Humans need each other, you will agree. The coroner is lonely, and this makes him maudlin.

"But I see he is not your problem. You are back here, safely in out of the rain."

Upon his return to the hotel, Mr. Bates had been informed that Detective Sergeant Xlong was waiting for him in the basement bar. He had changed out of his wet clothes and gone down.

"May I see your passport, please?"

"You just saw it yesterday."

"You are required to carry your passport at all times while a guest of the Republic."

"Instead of worrying about my passport, why don't you tell me where my son is?"

The policeman explained that such information was exactly what he hoped to provide. He and his fellow officers sympathized with Mr. Bates's dilemma. The father as responsible head of household, the father as concerned protector, the father as role model for the son, the father as warm bankroll, the father as principal figure in the ancestral history, the father as occupier of the time of the mother—all members of the police were familiar with the responsibilities of the thumb of the family, for these duties were listed in their handbook under: Relations, Human, Internal.

"Nevertheless, the law of the Republic requires that you surrender your passport upon demand."

"I realize that. But in all reasonableness, Detective Sergeant, you know it's in order."

"There are now complications."

"What complications?"

"I don't make the laws. I enforce them. Please produce your passport."

George Bates glared steadily at the policeman. He no doubt thought of him as little more than a nuisance, yet it would be difficult to determine precisely where to make a stand, at what point to refuse any further intimidation. It was essential not to be distracted from the goal of aiding his son.

Before his trip upriver, Philip had begun to spend most of his afternoons beneath the Royal Prince. Evenings were different. He wrote how it was always satisfying to watch evening sink into the tropics. The individual trees faded into a blank, uniform gloom the boy found reassuring. He said he liked the way the sky lost its pallor, gradually darkening like a wounded eyeball filling with blood.

Once he was certain the sun was down, he would climb up into the open, his head ringing with the alcohol he had consumed. He would hang back in the shadows, aware of the groups of languid women drifting down toward the river. Twilight was the time traditionally reserved for their pleasure. They bathed themselves in the dark water while their husbands and fathers remained at home, watching over the younger children and guarding the evening's meal against thieves.

On the night before leaving for upriver, Philip had had too much whiskey. He had fallen on the stairs and again on the street. The second time he had realized how unsteady he was and had leaned against the back wall of the hotel to rest. He wrote how serene the town had seemed to him at that moment. The incessant barking of the local dogs had become subdued, and a random pattern of dull yellow lights had glowed behind windows like clumps of burning hair.

He would have preferred to go down to the riverside and watch the women enjoy their hour of comfort, but he suspected that might be forbidden and so remained clinging to the shadows of the hotel.

A child had run toward him, a little girl about seven or eight, hurrying to catch up with the others on their way to the river. When she saw Philip, she stopped, frightened, then turned and scampered back toward her house.

Philip had followed her. The first building he checked was an empty shell, but the next had a pile of fresh rubbish in front of it, always an indication of human habitation. From where he was standing he couldn't see through the window, so he had just begun to move around to the side of the house when a door opened and an old lady limped out, leading the timid little girl by the hand.

Philip wrote how he had hesitated when he saw them. At the time, he'd had no sense that there was anything wrong in looking through someone's window. But there were police here, after all. What would he have explained to the fat hand holding a flashlight? That he was only curious how the people lived, not knowing how himself? That he was lonely? That he was a tourist, and thus to be forgiven any violations? That his fingertips were sucked toward light without his control?

Philip had abruptly stepped into the alley to pat the

child; he wasn't a monster. The moment she saw him, she burst into shouts of fear. He had stooped down to make himself smaller, clucking reassuringly. The old granny pushed the child toward his waiting arms. He asked if she would like some chocolate, despite the fact that he had none. The little girl became hysterical at the sight of his bared teeth. She began tearing at her granny, trying to escape.

"She's awfully shy, isn't she?" Philip had said, also growing frightened.

The granny had laughed as the child at last managed to work herself free. Without another look, she dashed down the length of the alley, her sarong clutched up around her hips and her bare legs flashing in the darkness.

Philip shoved his hands into his pockets. He wrote that he had suddenly become as self-conscious as a shy vivisectionist hiding the disassembled bodies of cats. The granny had turned and limped after the child, obviously amused. Philip waited under the heavy sky. He knew better than to try to follow them. There had been nothing for him to do, other than to try to take pleasure in the fact that the alley was deserted again. He wrote how at such moments he could feel the jungle night sucking at him like a huge, amorphous leech, and that this helped him to understand how nice it could be to be alone. He had never had much skill with human relationships.

"The photograph in this passport does not resemble you."

"On the contrary, it's a very good likeness. It was taken shortly before I left Los Angeles."

"This is your full name on this passport?"

"It is. And if you check the validation stamp in the visa section, you can see some of your name, too."

"It's not necessary to make clever suggestions, Mr. Bates. Humor is of little use in an investigation."

"I should be informed of the charges against my son in order to arrange for legal counsel."

"Counsel? Mice nipping at the ankles of the police. You will please think carefully before introducing such trouble-makers into an already complex situation.

"Now tell me the birth date of the owner of this passport."

"That's my passport and my birth date!"

"You're becoming annoyed, Mr. Bates. No doubt the weather here . . ."

"I'm perfectly calm. And ʻif you want things to go smoothly, you might begin by telling me exactly what crime you're investigating."

"Agreed, Mr. Bates, but which of two crimes has not yet been determined. Therefore . . ."

"What are the two?"

The policeman paused, surprised by Mr. Bates's sudden aggressiveness. He signaled toward the bartender.

"Please understand our need to be careful. The rebels are skillful at covert . . ."

"What crimes?"

"Homicide," the policeman replied sharply, "or the con-spiracy to commit homicide. I need hardly add that one of the two carries an extremely harsh penalty. With con-spiracy, a suspended sentence is possible. The malefactor might very likely be released to the custody of his father.

Therefore, any information you can give us as an aid to the investigation would directly benefit your son."

"Someone's been killed?"

"Has been killed, will be killed, is about to be killed, is being killed. . . . The investigation has its own innate rhythm, but at the moment, we would do well to proceed as if it could be hurried."

George Bates sat silently, ignoring the bartender, who waited for him to order something. Detective Sergeant Xlong mentioned that there was rarely any reason to become angry in such cases. He himself simply did his duty. From what he had been able to determine, there was, or was to be, a murder upriver. He had every desire to facilitate matters, but the process itself had become badly snarled. The obdurate coroner was now of primary importance. There had been no death certificate, and as the corpse was as yet unproduced—perhaps, indeed, still wandering through the world consuming food, oxygen, what have you—legally, no death. Thus, obviously, the investigation had dribbled into various difficulties. The unidentified victim was somewhere upriver, this seemed certain, although in which condition one could only speculate. Time was of the essence.

"One simple fact," Mr. Bates said in a sullen voice. "It appears that you yourself don't have Philip detained— directly, that is. Am I correct?"

He was. But the coroner must be pried from his inflexible position. Certificates had been floated in the past, but as Detective Sergeant Xlong had mentioned earlier, the bureaucracy was swollen with self-consciousness. To circumvent this deadlock, he had a suggestion. Would Mr.

Bates be willing to file a petition for a writ of habeas corpus as a friend of the police?

George Bates's eyes narrowed. He wondered if there was perhaps a fee for such a petition.

There was, as a matter of fact. The total amount was 200,000 *lolls*.

George Bates wondered if the policeman was the one authorized to handle such a transaction.

It so happened he was.

Mr. Bates had thought as much. "Then can we settle this matter without delay, once and for all?"

"That would be possible—for at least this step in the investigation, you understand."

He did. In return, he would expect to be told exactly where his son was.

The policeman scratched his ear. That would be difficult, but perhaps it could be arranged.

"Not good enough, Detective Sergeant. It must be guaranteed."

Again, the policeman seemed to be measuring George Bates. "Done," he agreed at last.

George Bates counted out twenty 10,000-*loll* notes while Detective Sergeant Xlong wrote a receipt on one of the scraps of paper he carried about for just such emergencies. He tried to attach the folded slip into Mr. Bates's passport with a drop of spittle, but that proved insufficiently adhesive. In the end, he had to leave it sticking out of the top like a bookmark.

"I have a junior officer of great determination. You have met him, as a matter of fact. He has not once had his boots off since the day of his elevation to the force. I will send him in pursuit of this question. We are sure of satisfaction."

George Bates handed over the pulpy mound of currency and remarked that he was very attentive to his duties.

"We of the police never sleep."

❖‹‹❖‹‹❖‹‹❖‹‹❖‹‹❖‹‹

"I found him with his vacuum tubes. He loves to watch the little worms of light."

Detective Sergeant Xlong climbed ponderously onto the barstool beside Mr. Bates. He apologized for having taken so long and swung his heavy pistol around in front of him to defend it against theft. Somewhere deep in the basement behind them a section of plaster fell with a sodden crash.

"The radio equipment is a gift from your government. He is obsessed with it, although he has been unable to coax out anything beyond a kind of white hiss, like sheets of water rushing over stones.

"When I explained to him what we wanted to know, he set out immediately."

The policeman observed his reflection in the mirror. He suggested that Mr. Bates might be brooding about misinformation Sprague had given him. Perhaps he would like to talk it over? Clear up the errors? No?

No problem; he was willing to wait.

The policeman wondered aloud if he seemed overly satisfied with himself. As a businessman and a father, Mr. Bates could surely appreciate the pleasure to be found in a job well done. Although misunderstandings bloomed like a thousand flowers, the police still managed to provide a measure of public safety.

Agreed, the recent history of the Republic was full of tales of violence, many of them set in the jungle surrounding the tin smeltery. They were badly exaggerated, however. The local people liked to repeat such nonsense. Excitement helped to keep their minds off the misery of poverty, as well as off the wretched weather. Sprague, as an informant, was unreliable because he was not properly disinterested.

"The weather, Mr. Bates, the weather—few glues work here. The smashed cup is broken forever."

"I haven't heard any stories."

"No? But some things may be less untrue than others. You should appreciate that we of the police can make use of what seems to be no more than random babblings. Everything, properly applied, has weight."

The bartender arrived with two cocktails similar to those Sprague had ordered earlier, although now garnished with globes of black gelatin impaled on toothpicks.

Detective Sergeant Xlong called Mr. Bates's attention to a barmaid passing with a bucket and mop. Sections of the basement bar had been destroyed in a terrorist bombing. Mr. Bates could understand why these areas were closed off as public hazards. If he listened carefully when the rains became heavy, he would hear the old hotel groan with its reawakened wounds. Avoid, it seemed to say, avoid.

But perhaps it was difficult for foreigners to appreciate forms of experience common to life in the jungle.

"It can be an unpleasant duty, Mr. Bates, picking over the bones of the dead for causes. We feel so after the fact. No wonder we get lonely."

George Bates did not understand.

"Prevention becomes . . ." the policeman said, then paused as if seeking an appropriate phrase.

Another sheet of plaster dropped with a sluggish gasp. The barmaid appeared at the far end of the main room, her stained white arms held out awkwardly before her like a pair of phosphorescent fish.

"Life," the detective sergeant said, and shook his head.

Philip wrote how he had lingered in that night alley, trying to remind himself where he was and why he was there, but a valve had closed and he was left with the sole sensation of streaming through his own body. What would it have been like to have had someone spying on his failure to befriend the little girl? A witness peeking from a darkened window would have seen nothing more than his hands still thrust innocently among the bits of money in his pants. No blame? Or just none recorded?

He wrote how he had tried to explain to himself why he did such a bad job with human affection. He was like something that hadn't sufficiently uncurled, like the tips of new ferns killed in a freeze, brown hooks gradually stiffening in the bleak morning light. He knew there was something others expected him to feel. He had no recollection of ever having felt it.

Quick black flecks of hunting bats had darted above his head like rubber fists. He had stood in the middle of the alley and wondered if it would be possible to snare one by stringing nets from roof to roof. He wrote that the few times his father's pain had flowed to the surface, his own mouth, too, had filled with the taste of metal, recalling his peculiar childhood habit of sucking on nails.

Turning back toward the hotel, he had told himself the town was small, the surrounding jungle dense and difficult to penetrate. The children would gradually become used to him. He might in the end even find one that would agree to act as a messenger, or guide, whatever.

And as for love, well, he was on vacation. Nor was he really interested in trapping bats.

"If you would care to go to her," said the policeman, indicating the distressed barmaid, "she undoubtedly knows a few sentences in your language."

"Why can't you understand that all I'm interested in is my son? You insist on ignoring my requests!"

Detective Sergeant Xlong glanced sadly at his thumbs. Haste was essential, agreed, but Mr. Bates did not take fully into account the necessity for thoroughness in an investigation. Sprague was not the simple clown he appeared. The police had had many bad experiences with him. He could produce documentation. Mr. Bates had perhaps had a taste of the fellow's devious nature. They would value his opinion. As he, Detective Sergeant Xlong, had mentioned earlier, cooperation was the great thing.

He could appreciate that George Bates was tired. His shoulders perhaps ached with exhaustion. Nevertheless, an understanding at this time would greatly simplify matters.

George Bates said flatly he had no intention of doing anything other than returning to his home with his son.

As far as he was concerned, the police were mistaken about Sprague.

"I'm surprised you defend him."

"I don't."

"He is of course your countryman."

"What are you selling now?"

"Mr. Bates, it is the duty of the police . . ."

"I've only expressed the opinion that he's harmless. I won't put up with this questioning!"

The policeman modestly looked down again. He claimed to appreciate loyalty in friendships. It was enough to make him wish that members of the police had the leisure to indulge themselves with friends. The shared bottle, tickets to a sporting contest, the recounting of an affair with a woman—he had heard of these pleasantries, although he himself had had no time for such amusements.

But Mr. Bates had not correctly understood the role Sprague may have played in this matter of his son. Why didn't Sprague accompany him upriver? Because of his sickness? No doubt. The fellow was far from healthy. But Mr. Bates may have noticed that stamina occasionally returned to him, and that even his limp could improve. It was true he had suffered a stroke, but it was also true that he had learned to manipulate his disability.

Why had he sent Philip upriver alone? If he were asked, the policeman would have to submit that it was because Sprague knew the adventure could only end in disaster. Why did he select Philip; had Mr. Bates wondered about that?

Detective Sergeant Xlong himself had not actually met

the young man in question, but did Mr. Bates have any reason to suspect that his son might be willing to undertake an unusually dangerous adventure? An adventure that might very well end in death?

Of course, legally, the druggist who sells poison to the suicide might be no more responsible than the fellow who twines the noose for the state; nevertheless . . .

George Bates's face had lost all color. He started to rise, but the policeman continued.

And why had Sprague sent his son off on a hopeless task? Did he suspect he could benefit either way? Could he possibly hope to profit from an investigation which led members of the police into the upriver jungle? Was there something or someone Sprague had his eye on? Philip was supposed to look around the smeltery, but was that *all* he was supposed to do? Victim or victimizer—for Sprague, Philip would serve equally well in either role.

"Painful questions, Mr. Bates. And as we of the police have so little information, it's hard to fasten anything more satisfying than these speculations to your son's case.

"But clearly, you can see that Sprague is at least an accessory. The problem remains, of course, to which crime?"

George Bates stared into his empty glass. He had been shaken.

In connection with Mr. Bates's son, the policeman went on, Sprague would be firmly pursued. He was involved.

The main question, he repeated, must be why Philip had consented to go. But no doubt Mr. Bates himself would be the one to answer that, for he was from a land of great psychological sophistication and would have a better understanding of motive than would an ignorant jungle policeman.

More plaster fell. The wall behind the bar had also bloated out and dark maps could be distinguished where seepage had reached the surface. George Bates stood and began to denounce the policeman, but his anger was so torpid, so sodden with hopelessness, that the first words of his complaint filled his mouth like lumps of wet dough.

Detective Sergeant Xlong plucked the shiny black sphere from his glass. It was the jellied egg of a reptile, the grainy shell soft and slippery from having been steeped in alcohol. Detective Sergeant Xlong wondered if Mr. Bates could distinguish the fetus wound inside, tangled as a knot.

"You see?" said the policeman, as if the fermented egg explained everything. It was always best to appreciate the pace of an investigation. Although there were times when it might be pressed, the wise officer remained tuned to its innate rhythms. He hoped Mr. Bates could appreciate that they were firmly on schedule. The night lay spread open before them, although Mr. Bates would probably use it for sleeping.

George Bates repeated that all he wanted was his son.

"Of course. There's no question about that. But you have nothing further you wish to tell me about Sprague?"

Mr. Bates shook his head.

"Very good. Perhaps we can understand each other after all. Here in the Republic, contexts shift. You would do well to attach yourself to a single proposition."

He wanted his son.

"You want your son. Perfectly natural. You want your son, and you want to go home. And you do not intend to involve yourself in the domestic affairs of this country?"

He did not.

"Then once my junior officer has determined the location of your son's detention, things should go forward smoothly.

"In the meantime, another drink perhaps? A nightcap as a guest of the police? You will have to admit at least that much, Mr. Bates, for you are truly a guest of the police."

❖❮❖❮❖❮❖❮❖❮❖❮❖❮❖❮❖❮❖❮

"Look at that beak!"

"Who? What?" George Bates had dozed off on his bed still fully clothed.

"Look at the extension on that neck!" Sprague said, tilting the cock forward and causing its head to stick out. "We call that 'reach.' And look at that eye! That eye is the eye of a cold-hearted killer! Give me a few days to get some blood in this baby, and we'll be ready to kick ass!"

"What are you talking about? Shut the door!"

"When I first caught sight of this fellow, I stopped and said to myself: C. K., you and him have a future. He's scrawny and pecked up, and full of vinegar—just like me! All he needs is a little coaching, and we'll have us a champion!

"And I don't mind saying I owe it all to you, George. You don't care if I call you George, do you, George? On account of how I was down, but you gave me new heart. C. K. Sprague is grateful, and not afraid to show it. Consider yourself cut in."

George Bates climbed off his bed to shut the door. "There's a policeman looking for you."

"Sure. Boss of the local bulls, an old acquaintance of mine. I told you before. We even did some business a few years back, although I don't expect he mentioned it. He's part of this situation we got.

"But listen, George, this is important. I think I got a line on how we can do that problem of yours. We just got to get up there and . . ."

"I don't want to know," Mr. Bates said crossly. "And take that chicken out of here."

"What?" Sprague's head jerked up. "What?" He thrust his face forward. Flecks of gristle and bits of greasy wool were embedded in his beard, as if he'd combed supper trash from his lips and halfway through lost track of it.

"Don't you *ever* call this a chicken! It's a cock, a *fighting* cock! You got to learn the proper terminology if you're going to make it in sports."

"Are you crazy? Are you completely . . ."

"Listen, George, the trouble with you is you take everything too seriously. What are you worried about? That cop likely couldn't find his own feet. It's his family's fault things got so out of control around here in the first place.

"But like I said, I got a few good ideas on how to help you. I don't want to go into the details just yet, but this cock is the way in. If we work together, we'll get what we want. It's so simple, I don't see why I didn't think of it this afternoon."

"Would you please leave?"

"No, wait, now listen. We're both getting stepped on by the same boot. You know where your boy is hiding is somewhere around that smeltery, am I right?"

George Bates paused with his hand on the doorknob. "How did you know?"

"Why do you think I'm here? Soon as I found out how he'd escaped, I started putting two and two together. The whole thing's a setup. That geologist figured I was getting too close to his smeltery and . . ."

"What are you talking about? Escaped? Who? The geologist is the one who was murdered, or who is going to be, or, I mean . . ."

"Not at all! Lies, tricks to suck you in, George. Why else would there be all this trouble? It's that cop. He's got a brother named Plo-xlong who has always been sympathetic to the rebels. Now they say he's at the smeltery. Two plus two, George."

"You mean you think Detective Sergeant Xlong is . . ."

"No, now, did I say that? Not necessarily your direct involvement. This Xlong family they got is a real mess. You could hold up a piece of gear and ask what it was, and no two of them would have the same opinion. I told you the geologist's wife was one of them. Well, even though they don't get along, they're still family, if you know what I mean.

"George, I wish you wouldn't look so surprised all the time. If we're going to drain the boys upriver, you're going to have to look like you know what you're doing even though you don't."

"They said Philip disappeared, so I . . ."

"Look, don't worry about that. We'll burn that bridge when we cross it. What we need now is an excuse to poke around up there. He's it," Sprague said, stroking the cock fondly. "You put up the cash and I put up the time and talent. We'll call ourselves 'Sprague and Associates, Pit Sports, Incorporated'—although not out loud yet, you understand. On account of my present poor personal relationships with the police, I mean."

"But why not just go up by boat? Couldn't we . . ."

"Right, George. Great idea! Maybe hire a band, just so there's no doubt what we're up to. No sense in not giving everybody an equal chance to shoot at us!"

"But . . ."

"Boy, you are *green*, George."

"But I've told you I don't want to . . ."

"Okay! I hear you! C. K. Sprague sniffs out a touchy situation when he sees one. I always told you I was cool. You be the silent bankroll until we get upriver. Somebody asks if I know you, I say, 'Who? George who? Can't say I've had the, you know, pleasure.' Like that, cool.

"I can dig it. Like the Mafia, those sons of bitches. How they paid the ticket for when Kennedy got it. You know? Them and the CIA and Dow Chemical."

"Dow Chemical?"

"Right. Did you know Dow Chemical has a secret contract with the Pentagon to poison every man, woman, and child in North America? Documented fact!"

"That's ridiculous!"

"Damn right it is, those two-timing, double-dealing . . ."

"No, I mean . . ."

"Stockpiled in canisters around the country ready to go into the drinking water soon as Nixon gives the word."

"Nixon? Haven't you even heard that he . . ."

"It's what's holding back the revolution!"

"Look, just get out of here now. We'll talk about it tomorrow."

"Sure. No problem. Here, I made this list here with the estimate of the costs. Here, you can read that here. Can you read that? My pencil was so short I couldn't hardly hold it and then the lead, it broke, and I didn't have my knife and had to chew away the wood with my teeth, which aren't so good these days anymore."

"What's all this? 'Training dummy, two hundred thousand *lolls;* fighting spurs, two sets at five hundred thousand *lolls* each; food; food for handler; whiskey ration; ap—, ap—.' What's this? '*Appropriate*'? You don't spell 'appropriate' like that. What's this? 'Appropriate clothes suitable for trainer'? The total here comes out to over two million *lolls!*"

"You don't have to put it all up at one time, of course. Just enough to get us started . . ."

"Out!"

"No, wait. There's this rotten wall in this abandoned basement we're going to make our temporary training headquarters. It's right under the old pit. I'll take you down later and show you around. It's not much but we can fix it up some. Anyway, it has this rotten wall. You can see it's full of mice. Which is why I chose it. And also on account of how the legal owner is dead, and . . ."

"Out! Now!"

"Right, I'm going. Anyway, you can see for yourself how these mice are in there, so I'm going to start him on a training diet tomorrow, or whenever I can catch one; a mouse, I mean. It's his diet needs work now. His previous handler didn't know shit about that nutri—, nutra—, unh, food—like what you eat."

"I *know* what food is! Now would you please . . ."

"Sure. But now about this previous handler . . ."

"His previous handler?" George Bates said, working Sprague into the doorway. "Where did you get him?"

"Fellow down the line, like I was going to say. But not a word about that yet. The deal hasn't been finally . . ."

"You mean you didn't pay for this bird?"

". . . concluded. But it'll come out of the first purse, good as my word—if not better. C. K. Sprague has had experience with debts and knows how to make the most of them."

George Bates had managed to work him into the hall. At the last moment Sprague pivoted and shoved the cock in the closing doorway. Mr. Bates and the bird were eye to eye. He wasn't about to touch it.

"I need a break, George!"

Mr. Bates pushed against the door. The cock pecked viciously at his hand.

"Your boy's on the lam, which is what I do mostly! It's like I got experience. I can save him!"

Still leaning against the door, George Bates bent down to pry off a shoe.

"This is my last chance! You understand? I'm stuck here with that cop. He's going to pin something on me!"

Mr. Bates took a swing at the cock's head, but missed.

"And I didn't tell him to shoot anybody."

George Bates stopped. "What? Shoot?"

"Yeah, well," said Sprague, suddenly wary. "On account of how he's out to get me; the cop, I mean."

"What do you mean, 'shoot'? So Philip *did* shoot someone? Was it the geologist?"

"Well, now, no. I don't know; now, no, you know how that Philip was sort of upset about things and he . . ."

George Bates yanked open the door and shoved Sprague against the far wall. The man's bad leg buckled under him. Mr. Bates stepped back as Sprague folded like a rag onto the hall carpet.

"It hurts!" Sprague cried, thrashing against the wall. "It hurts! It hurts!"

The freed cock flapped past George Bates's ankles and perched on the lip of his open suitcase. Head up, wings out, it challenged him to a fight.

Mr. Bates helped Sprague get to his feet.

"Whiskey," Sprague moaned, "to kill the pain."

"But you're not hurt, are you?"

Sprague dragged himself to a chair. "Thought I was a goner sure," he said, brightening as George Bates produced a bottle. "It just goes to show that it doesn't pay not to pay attention to your good health when you got it. Not that I got it, mind you."

"Listen," George Bates said, eyeing the cock, which was strutting obnoxiously across his fresh underwear. "I didn't . . ."

"Nope! My own fault. Just caught me off guard. Although for an old guy, you pack a pretty good punch."

"But I didn't hit you!"

"Didn't mean that exactly. You're just tougher than you look. Wiry, like they say."

The cock began scratching at Mr. Bates's socks.

"I've never been involved in anything so . . ."

"First time for everything, George. But here." Sprague offered the bottle. "Don't let me hog it. Particularly as how you won and all."

"But it wasn't like that!"

"Nothing to be ashamed of, George. Better man won, that's all; better luck next time, like they say."

"Next time?"

Detective Sergeant Xlong had at last reached his little friend's table. Placing his body face down on the familiar wood, he suggested wringing strokes to loosen his knotted calves. He knew Moule liked him to give her advice. He assumed it helped her to restrain herself from rushing directly to the root.

The policeman suspected there would be action tonight. His body had become so strung with anticipation, several critical sections were almost cramped from tension. Without little Moule, he might become incapacitated.

Her thumbs bit deeply into his gastrocnemius. He told himself how fond he was of her hands. Sensations flooded his body. He hoped it was good for her, too.

Tonight, then, he might be required to act. Feelers had been extended. Probes had had their wet canvas covers skinned back—it was enough to make him long for something celebratory, a few slivers from a Christmas song. His junior officers prowled in pairs, their faces blackened, the fresh leather joints in their equipment lubricated with tallow. "Police!" He muttered, forming little bubbles in the corners of his lips and causing Moule to pause in her rhythmic kneading. Did she wonder if that meant he wanted her to remove her brassiere? She didn't ask.

The policeman hoped George Bates had begun to appreciate that he was truly honest, and that the money Mr. Bates had assumed to be simple extortion actually had been aimed toward a clogged bureaucratic conduit which would, in fact, loosen. One wanted a mind for flow here. Investigations were fluid. Hard facts not seated in probability could cause constriction. One struggled to relax.

Moule sat back. She confessed her thumbs had become numb.

"Emotion?"

She shook her head. No. She was only tired.

Detective Sergeant Xlong did not question her. He knew women could be moody.

"He's not the Pearl, you understand. We'll take losses."

The cock was now roosting on Mr. Bates's jacket.

"We just pretend to be a couple of old cockfighters working the upriver pits?"

"Hell, George, they know me. If I try to hit those pits openly, they'll sit on their dough. But with you as a front . . ."

George Bates would have begun to recognize that Sprague's focus was on the geography of the situation. Events were irrelevant. He was as interested in the ruse as in whatever it was designed to mask. He talked of cockfights upriver barred to him, of rubes betting on birds armed only with bamboo spurs. Money was up there, piles of it. It would be criminal not to go up and grab some.

"And the smeltery?"

"And then just walk around the smeltery and kind of look at it. Figure out who's doing what. Once we know their strength, we can guess their weakness. Once we know where to touch them . . ."

"Touch who?"

". . . your boy's as good as sprung. Huh? Who?"

"Who?"

"Huh?"

"You think he's being held?"

"Held, hiding out, it's the same thing."

"It is?"

"Sure! What he isn't is free, isn't it?"

"Well . . ."

"Told you that geologist was a tricky bastard."

"I thought he was the one that was . . ."

"Dead? Did I say that? I never said he was anything but upriver pumping tin. You listen to that cop too much, that's what you do!"

The policeman rolled up onto one elbow. "Tell me," he said. Moule's fingers fluttered to her neck. "Tell me," he said again. She shook her head. It was nothing; she was being silly.

The policeman studied her. It came to his attention that she had thoughts and emotions all her own. He had always experienced her as an extension of himself. He could now clearly make out smudged mascara, a trace of lipstick, beads of perspiration on her nose. For the first time, he thought he saw her as an object separate from himself. Was she pretty? He had no idea. He wondered if this was what people meant when they said they were falling in love. He rolled back onto his belly. The subject would

73

have to wait. He suggested she compose herself by drinking a glass of cold water.

"Upriver," said Sprague, his eyes narrowing in anticipation. "Upriver, that's where I'll be, just as soon as I get a little muscle on that fellow's bones and a little hatred in his heart."

"I?" George Bates said, sinking to the foot of his bed. "Then you don't expect me to go?"

"Don't you want to go?"

"I don't know."

"You don't know what?"

"If I should want to go or not."

"What kind of a goddamn thing to say is that?"

"It doesn't seem to have any point, and . . ."

"Point? Profit's the point!"

". . . and it seems dangerous."

"Of course it seems dangerous! It *is* dangerous. It's *supposed* to be dangerous. How else are we going to get the other guys to loosen up enough so we can get in and get them?"

"It doesn't make any sense. We'd probably just be causing Philip more trouble."

"Life is trouble, George. The trick is to make it not be your own. You don't understand how things work around here. Don't you listen to me when I explain it to you?"

"I *do* listen; that's the problem."

"The problem is that you want to get your son back, isn't it?"

George Bates nodded.

"Well, all right. It's settled."

"What's settled?"

"What the problem is!" Sprague said expansively, and, pushing with his hands, came up out of his chair. He stood to test his bad leg. Although it still dragged, it didn't seem worse than before.

"You know what we need?"

George Bates shook his head.

"A good name for him."

George Bates didn't say anything.

"Listen, you're always thinking all the time; how about a name for him? Seeing as how you're a partner."

"But I haven't . . ."

"Something rotten is best. Something vicious, so he can take pride in it. Like in that movie *Texas Chain Saw Massacre,* how they did it there. Did you see it? It never made it here, of course, nothing good ever does. But a guy off a boat told me all about it. I guess it must've been something to see. You see it, George? It must've been in L.A. Hell, George, L.A., you got everything in L.A.

"Anyway, there was this guy, see, and he had this chain saw, see, and at the beginning, he . . ."

"Don't tell me!"

"Sure, George. Anyway, the name's good, right? How about if we called him the Chain Saw Massacrer? What do you think?"

"Rather awkward, isn't it?"

"Awkward? No, hell, no, George, there're lightweight models now; a kid could use one."

George Bates scraped some money into a pile.

"Hey, there, be careful there, you're dropping it on the floor!"

"I can't . . ."

75

"No, that's okay, George; I'll pick it up. Boy, you sure get a funny look on your face sometimes. You ought to do something about that."

Mr. Bates turned back toward the cock in time to see it squirt a single white line down the front of his jacket.

Sprague crammed the money into his pockets. He asked George Bates if he wanted some sort of receipt or contract. George shook his head no; he was tired; he just wanted to go to bed.

"Sure," said Sprague, collecting his bird. "Everybody needs sleep.

"But you know one thing, how at the end of that movie this guy said that guy cut . . ."

George Bates closed the door in his face.

❖〈〈❖〈〈❖〈〈❖〈〈❖〈〈❖〈〈

Detective Sergeant Xlong stood alone in the deserted street. His breath was shallow; his body was drained. Had he disappointed Moule? Perhaps, but it was a night for duty. He wondered if George Bates had any sense of his son wandering lost in the upriver jungles, a pistol heavy as midnight in his pocket. He suspected he didn't.

The policeman lingered in the humid air, hoping to pick up the echo of a shot. His intuition had tugged at him, telling him to beware the touch of murder in the air.

But nothing happened; he was premature.

Moule's light went out. The street was now perfectly dark. The citizens safely slept, snug in the knowledge that their policeman was guarding them. Detective Sergeant Xlong walked up the middle of the street, enjoying the crunch of asphalt beneath his boots. He liked the town best when it was empty. It seemed neatest to him when there were only buildings. How nice it might be to have the place without the people, although of course that would make his own role as protector somewhat contradictory.

Some of his men had no doubt curled up under bushes to await the sunrise; but others should still be in motion, obeying orders, cutting through layers of foliage, waking citizens and asking questions.

It seemed unlikely that any of them would actually find the foreigner's son. Perhaps in the morning he might confide in George Bates, explain to him how he could have been mistaken about Philip.

He checked the lock on the door of the bank. What was it Moule always seemed to be wanting? Whenever he was about to depart, she became watery.

He thought of how his hammock cords would part under the weight of his buttocks; he was tempted.

Or perhaps he might not tell George Bates, for both the act of confiding and the neglect to do so were successful police techniques.

HOW TO BEHAVE HERE

"Yes, Mr. Bates, a bicycle ride through the tropical forest—I've always suspected this would be one of the thrills of tourism. I'm pleased you've decided to enjoy yourself. But haven't you perhaps been misinformed? The greatest dangers to jungle trail travel are not the grassy cannonballs of elephant excrement. Agreed, to hit one of these terrors with the front wheel of one's bicycle would be to invite a nasty fall, for the inside of the sphere is quite slippery—as is, I suppose, the inside of the elephant. Nevertheless, it's my duty to inform you that among the many hazards here in the jungle, these are not the most feared."

George Bates had cycled out from town, intending, perhaps, to use the cool of the morning for some preliminary reconnoitering. Still attempting to establish a harmonious relationship, Detective Sergeant Xlong made no mention of the covert nature of Mr. Bates's act. The foreigner, however, had become even less responsive than the night before. Was he annoyed by the rudeness of the squad of soldiers he had blundered into? The policeman was unsure. Perhaps Mr. Bates suspected they had trailed him from town.

Detective Sergeant Xlong recalled how his little friend from Hong Kong had been amazed that the interior of the jungle was relatively easy to move through. On a recent outing Moule had plunged into the shadows only to stop and clap her wet palms together, overcome by the swollen insistence of life in the gloom. "Moss beds," she murmured, dragging her fingertips across the dark surfaces she found both spongy and suggestive. "Huge liverworts everywhere!" She stroked frond edges. "They're as thick as lips! And look at the seedlings of the big trees! How long and hard they are! Their bark is so smooth, Bobo! And see how doggedly they cling to life!"

There was too little light. The policeman had explained that they were waiting for their parent to die. The meager ration of sunflecks which filtered down from above was barely enough to sustain life. Without a light-space to grow into, they would remain stunted forever.

"But look at them! They're filled with hope!"

Such was the familiar result of starvation in its early stages, Detective Sergeant Xlong had remarked.

"Where's your sense of romance, Bobo?"

He had kicked at an immense mushroom the size and consistency of a sodden pillow. His boot toe yellowed with spores, but he had made no further reply. When Moule later told him he had been too reserved, he explained that he liked her better in her room. She had given him an odd look and added that she always learned a lot from his explanations.

George Bates had been pedaling aggressively. He appeared energetic for the first time since his arrival. Perhaps the uncertainties of Philip's alleged crime had stiffened him. He might even have concluded that the ambiguity of the situation offered him an opportunity to manipulate members of the police—an error that could impede the investigation.

Mr. Bates set his jaw. Clearly, his anger was lit. He stared at the squad of soldiers standing stupidly behind Detective Sergeant Xlong and did not try to hide his contempt. The policeman, too, observed his men. Their faces were slack; their uniforms were splattered with mud and grease. Although they had been provided with individual bunks, he knew they slept piled on each other in one corner of their barracks.

"They're young," he said without conviction.

A fly walked down the cheek of the nearest militiaman. It didn't sting him; he saw no reason to slap it. Detective Sergeant Xlong felt the weariness that came with comprehension. He could see the squad through George Bates's eyes. It was at this point that he was most vulnerable. He restrained his sense of disappointment with difficulty; further adjustments might be required of him.

He squared his cap. He appreciated that Mr. Bates had no receptors for the tensions that sucked on him, for the messages trickling from upriver, the veiled hints of a homicide as yet uncompleted, delayed, fumbled even—but one still there, still ticking upriver as faint as the heartbeat of a fetus beneath the drum of the mother's belly—a legitimate homicide, although one to which he, the policeman, was as yet unable to fix person, place, time, or the essential question of premeditation.

Detective Sergeant Xlong wondered how long George Bates would refuse to speak. Over their heads, epiphytic plants clotted the canopy. Should he have pointed out this curiosity to the foreigner as an indication of the cooperation to be found in the natural world? Attached to the trunks and branches of trees, to the stems of lianas, even directly to some of the larger leaves, everywhere things were growing together, connected with tangles of aerial roots, squeezing each other, surviving anyplace there was sufficient sunlight. He could share with George Bates how the fecundity had caused his little friend from Hong Kong to raise her powerful hands up toward the brightness far above them, extending herself to her full height as she began to rotate—emitting, in sharp, breathless grunts of pleasure, the word in her language for the splendor of life.

George Bates's face was pinched shut. The policeman had little hope that he could be taught to appreciate the jungle. Mr. Bates would no doubt reject what he thought of as his son's hunger for the bizarre, for the distraction of lush and unwholesome air. Detective Sergeant Xlong knew it would never occur to Mr. Bates that one might attach one's inner sense of dislocation to a matching environment—a conception that, once he had formulated it, filled him with satisfaction. Officers of the police had every reason to employ such speculations, if for no other use than to bolster themselves against the futile floundering that inevitably accompanied the absence of crime.

The welt beneath George Bates's left eye was beginning

81

to turn green. He had said nothing about it. The offending soldier squatted alone on the perimeter and hung his head while a junior officer berated him. One didn't hit the foreigner, particularly where it would show. A long smear of trail mud discolored Mr. Bates's trousers. He wouldn't mention that, either. The message of his bitter silence was clear. He no doubt expected nothing less than casual brutality from the police. Detective Sergeant Xlong suspected the foreigner would enjoy his indignation and wear his injury like a flag.

"I suppose you realize we of the police are responsible for public safety. If someone were to stray too far from town, it would be our duty to rescue him."

George Bates's face filled with scorn. He said he was sure the citizens were appropriately grateful.

Detective Sergeant Xlong pretended to examine the treetops, intending to indicate his regret at the clumsy way his men had handled George Bates. Philip had written with enthusiasm about the jungle canopy—how in contrast to the dank forest floor, the upper layers were filled with sunlight. Wonderful creatures spent their entire lives up there—arboreal pangolins and tarsiers, hornbills and gibbons and Asiatic climbing rats, and even an occasional slow loris, all fighting with each other for a little place to call home, a little privacy, a little dignity, a little bite of something to eat.

Philip insisted life here was like living underwater, a condition he had often felt before but never experienced quite so clearly. A branch would occasionally break off and fall crashing through layers of foliage, peeling off apes and birds until it landed at one's feet, a piece of already rotting wood—perhaps decorated with the grinning death's-heads of orchids; or even, although much more rarely, still wound with a snake that would soon be a scrounger's meal.

Things dropped here, Philip wrote. The basic direction was down—what he had always wanted to express but had never known how. He claimed to be like a person living at the bottom of a well. He got what fell on him.

"But perhaps it is I who have misunderstood? You have merely come to visit one of the ruined temples? You have decided to follow my advice and enjoy your stay in the Republic? I approve of that. As your friend and your protector, I second an act of public tourism. You will be the first to admit that the investigation is the proper affair of the police. Thus the problem that you are very far from town could be explained as an accident. You have overshot your mark. You didn't realize there are temples nearer, many with remarkable carvings."

Wisps of damp hair fell into Mr. Bates's eyes. He lifted a hand to clear them away. Instead of replying to the policeman's remarks, he mounted his bicycle and abruptly pushed past the temporary roadblock.

The soldiers were caught by surprise. The detective sergeant knew that his soldiers were always caught by surprise. Each morning at daybreak, he saw their faces crowded in the barracks' windows, snorting with wonder.

Detective Sergeant Xlong trotted behind Mr. Bates's bicycle. The trail ahead was mostly mud. The foreigner would soon become mired.

"You don't appreciate my concern!"

"There's no law against cycling in the forest, is there?"

"Law? Between friends? But you have noticed I've asked you nothing about this bicycle."

"It's rented!" George Bates exclaimed, pushing through the brush that crowded the outside of the track. "I can show you the rental agreement! The revenue stamp affixed to the rental contract! The bicycle rental tax receipt! And the extra revenue stamp affixed, just in case," he panted, "to that!"

"Something's troubling you, Mr. Bates."

"Something? I've been brutally assaulted by that, that troglodyte you sent after me!"

"He feels as bad about this as . . ."

"Don't touch my handlebars! I don't know how; but somehow, somewhere, I'm going to file a complaint!"

The soldiers slogged after them, dragging their rifles at awkward angles and making no effort not to splatter mud all over themselves. The policeman sighed. He wondered for a moment what it would be like to have men one could trust with live ammunition. He could see that George Bates's scalp was livid with rage; he might be in danger of some sort of attack. The day Detective Sergeant Xlong had held so much hope for had begun very inauspiciously.

The sky was filling with clouds; it was time for the first morning rain. Detective Sergeant Xlong slowed his jogging. Mr. Bates pressed on obdurately through the deepening mud. The policeman halted his soldiers and instructed his junior officer to line them up. George Bates's obstinacy was not the proper lesson for them at this moment.

"The weather!" he shouted toward the foreigner's back, but gained no reply.

He turned his full attention to his men. What had they learned about the proper preparation of a roadblock? They glanced at each other; they had already forgotten.

"Nothing?" he demanded.

"Have it in the mud?" a militiaman suggested, causing the others to snicker.

Clearly, patience was one of the fundamental requirements for the officers of the police.

❖(❖(❖(❖(❖(❖(❖(❖(❖(❖(

"You're . . . You're . . ."

The policeman looked at his feet. George Bates returned to wrenching at his bicycle wheel; it only worked more deeply into the mire. Detective Sergeant Xlong had intended to help him, but perhaps a few more moments of rage might aid Mr. Bates in getting past his unsociability.

The detective sergeant hunkered down. Two of his men began quarreling behind him; his junior officer silenced them. Detective Sergeant Xlong explained that as elephants sometimes used these trails to haul logs to the river, it was not safe here.

"In the evening they are apt to be clumsy due to exhaustion," the policeman mumbled.

"Do you think I'm going to stay here all day?"

Detective Sergeant Xlong was only doing his duty in warning Mr. Bates. The foreigner stared at him. Although his face was still stubborn, the policeman thought he could detect the first traces of doubt.

"There are cobras here, too. A great many can be found in the ruined temples. The rebels, for example, are frequent victims of these snakes, or so our reports tell us."

Mr. Bates continued to eye the policeman.

"Thus you can understand how our responsibilities for the safe handling of the people in our jurisdiction cause us to . . ."

"Safe handling?"

"You can appreciate that if someone came here determined to act in opposition to our principles, our soldiers might become confused."

"I don't give a damn about your soldiers, or your rebels, or your principles, or anything else in this miserable little country!"

"Mr. Bates, I've tried to explain to you how . . ."

"This is pointless!"

"Being excluded, Mr. Bates, is a bitter lesson for them. Please understand that the complications involved in your son's situation may be partly seen as stemming from our premature grasping . . ."

"Premature? I demand you tell me where my son is!"

Detective Sergeant Xlong wondered if he should confess that conflicting reports on that very question were what had drawn him into the jungle. Instead, he turned his attention to the bicycle wheel. Mud oozed to just beneath the hub. Never had he seen anything so badly bogged. Mr. Bates's son was believed to be wandering through the upriver jungles, a black pistol concealed in his pocket. Someone surely was going to be shot, may have been shot already. Mr. Bates's anger did nothing to ease the situation.

"Perhaps if you lifted here, at the fork, and I pulled at the wheel?"

George Bates abruptly climbed off his bicycle. Detective Sergeant Xlong tried to explain that new problems were arising at every juncture. It was all the police could do to make sense of the bits of information that came to them. George Bates interrupted, livid with indignation.

"I only brought a few thousand *lolls*," he said, "as there's nothing to buy in the jungle."

"Mr. Bates, you . . ."

"To say nothing of the fact that thick wads of money swell with the humidity!"

Detective Sergeant Xlong's smile folded into an expression of sadness. Mr. Bates's insistence on misunderstanding his motives was taking its toll. If he were attacked by a cobra, would he know what to do? No, he would not. He was too far from town. There were suitable ruins within the lips of the police perimeter. Such solitary adventuring was dangerous. He was not to assume that responses developed in his homeland would apply here. Had it not occurred to him that the difficulties his son now faced might be the result of heedless thrill seeking? No, the policeman agreed, raising his hand, the word *thrill* might be incorrect in this case; *distraction* seeking, say, might be better. Nevertheless, there were those upriver who had not enjoyed lessons on the sanctity of the human condition. Why couldn't Mr. Bates understand this?

One of the soldiers came behind George Bates and bent to sniff thoughtfully at the rear tire of his bicycle. When he shifted his attention to George Bates's knees, Detective Sergeant Xlong drove him away with a sharp grunt.

The detective sergeant's disappointment with George Bates faded. He sighed, smiled again, and scratched at an insect bite inflaming the back of his fist. Gradually he became confidential, almost obsequious. The squad would remove the bicycle voluntarily. Mr. Bates need not ask. Was there something further he could do for him? Perhaps their relationship had grown too one-dimensional? He placed a familiar hand on the front of the bicycle and gazed into Mr. Bates's face. Couldn't he buy him a drink? He knew a little place the foreigner hadn't seen yet. They could send the militiamen into upriver swamps and be done with them, he continued, aware that the blade of such a betrayal would later find him but unable to contain his enthusiasm at the prospect of communication. There were things he wanted to tell Mr. Bates. In his opinion, political misunderstanding could be seen as stemming from the fact that people did not come together in fellowship often enough.

"Harmony, that's the great thing. Two strong right arms locked together sharing—eating out of the same pot, marching in the same boots, setting examples for the same woman, lubricating the trigger mechanism on the same rifle—harmony."

George Bates stared at the policeman but said nothing. What did friends do in Mr. Bates's country? Sports? Games? Did Mr. Bates like to play cards? Detective Sergeant Xlong himself had no experience, but he had heard people in the West enjoyed such pastimes. If Mr. Bates needed a partner at cards, he would attempt to learn. There were rules, were there not? They could be easily memorized by one whose mind had been honed on the handbook of the police. After that, it would be merely a matter of adopting the correct strategy, would it not?

"Rules." The policeman repeated the word, rolling it lovingly in his mouth. "When my elder brother died, my family fell apart. Our cassava plants withered; our pigs sickened and grew thin. I had been at home in the jungle; but at his death, I was excluded. You can perhaps appreciate why I felt grateful to the police for their rules."

"Detective Sergeant, I'm wet and I'm chilled and . . ."

"You don't understand. In my case, there isn't just duty. There is also affection. Imagine my pain if you too should be killed while under my jurisdiction. You have not . . ."

"Then someone was killed?"

"I have always been careful to suggest that by 'killed' I might merely be indicating that an action which would logically end in a killing had been launched. Your friend Sprague . . ."

George Bates kicked his bicycle a vicious shot. He slogged off down the muddy path, his hands jammed angrily into his pockets. Detective Sergeant Xlong's soldiers gazed at him in amazement. Clearly, he had failed to communicate.

"I'm not leaving!" Mr. Bates shouted from a bend in the trail. "You can stall all you want, but I'm not leaving without my son."

"We don't want you to leave. We like you."

"You think I don't know you're hiding something? You think I don't know about your brother?"

"My brother?" Detective Sergeant Xlong removed his cap to examine the stains in the sweatband.

"I've heard talk—from Sprague, of course, I don't deny it. Understand? I *don't* deny it!"

"Sprague . . ."

"Is not important, but there's still something to what he said."

"On a witness stand, he . . ."

"This isn't a trial!"

The policeman firmly replaced his cap. He held his hands out, palms up in a simple gesture of acquiescence. He could now realize that he had no choice but to take Mr. Bates into his confidence. Should they say lunch? On the veranda at one?

"Lunch?"

In order to present an explanation of how things were different here. Mr. Bates would want to understand the base on which their culture was founded.

"Lunch!"

Could he, for example, appreciate that they thought of the cobra as their grandfather? And that this was one of the basic binding agents that held them together as a people?

"Lunch . . . ?"

Naga was their word for the cobra. His daughter had married a prince from beyond the sea, and their children became the people of this Archipelago. When a woman has a baby, she gives some of her milk to the *naga* so he will protect the baby.

"What are you *talking* about?"

Mr. Bates was perhaps wondering if the snake nursed directly from her nipple. Such an idea would be seen as

THREE: *How to Behave Here*

bizarre. A small dish was employed for the ritual, and a safe distance.

George Bates glanced about, bewildered. Detective Sergeant Xlong's soldiers crowded up behind him, bumping each other as they pushed forward to see.

"Each of them was once a child—malnourished, no doubt, diseased, but nevertheless a child whose mother paused in her suckling long enough to fulfill our ancestral charm."

George Bates looked at the militiamen. Was he struggling against disdain? It was clearly his turn to reconcile himself with where he was and what he could do about it.

"I suppose you're going to tell me the protected child is never bitten?"

Mr. Bates had not fully understood. But his irony was so drained of its previous bitterness that the policeman felt he had begun to arrive.

"Frequently bitten, bitten and killed; particularly vulnerable are these members of the militia who spend so much time in high grass."

"Then what's the point?"

Detective Sergeant Xlong felt calmer. Did George Bates sincerely want an answer? It seemed possible enough to proceed. He told him that even though the people were killed, they continued to revere the *naga*. They maintained faith in the order of things despite evidence to the contrary.

"So you do nothing when he kills you?" George Bates said, his voice showing his fatigue. "You think I can't understand that what you do around here is nothing?

I've been here for two days, and that what you do is nothing is . . ."

"Nothing? You're unfair," the policeman said, relieved that Mr. Bates had returned his attention to general complaints. "Perhaps it seems that way to you, but it's an accident when it happens. Death doesn't surprise us."

"That's all very well to say."

"If your son doesn't die here, he'll die somewhere else."

"You're going to tell me now people die? Very profound!"

Detective Sergeant Xlong felt the muscles of his face begin to stiffen into a grimace. He fought to control the spasm.

"And if you don't die here, you will die somewhere else, too. Nevertheless, it is my job to prevent both your son and now you from placing your deaths here."

"Then get me my son!"

"We will help each other," the policeman said, his lips numb.

George Bates shook his head slightly, but did not look up at the policeman. He would insist on retaining his son for himself alone as long as possible. A compromise might be appropriate here. Detective Sergeant Xlong recalled how Moule had puzzled him by suggesting that his idea of frankness was beyond the range of most people. He'd wondered if what she'd recognized wasn't simply the essence of the police.

The policeman made no mention of the impulsiveness characteristic of the unhappy young. He repeated that he had every intention of doing what he could to help Mr. Bates with his son. Mr. Bates, for his part, should make an effort to learn to rely upon the police. Detective Sergeant Xlong had an orderly mind. When he was taught to lace his boots, the ugliness of a skipped eyelet had been stressed—a lesson he bore to this day. He would proceed, then, in accordance with accepted police practices. Mr. Bates's insistence on adventuring in the jungle could only delay the investigation.

"If you only trusted us . . ." he said, then drew himself up to his full height and raised his arms above his head to loosen his shoulders. Some of the men would be detached to escort Mr. Bates back to town. This was not a gesture; this was a fact. They would be together again at one, as agreed. Surely the veranda would be more convivial than the basement bar, to say nothing of this swamp.

"Convivial?" George Bates echoed, making a final, perhaps conciliatory effort at irony.

"I may have the wrong word. I learned my English from books—and from missionaries whose patience was poor because their hearts were clogged.

"Forgiveness, Mr. Bates, that's the great thing. When I think of those missionaries, I remember how badly my family has been wounded."

But enough of this, the policeman determined abruptly. It was time for them to part. He turned to issue commands. Duty, for him, began with the shortening of distances. The unexpected display of force was a popular technique with the police, as was the expected. For rewards, they made do with the moment the probing hand found the wet skin of the offender.

There were unanswered questions concerning motive.

Had Mr. Bates any idea where Sprague could be reached? None? No matter. The policeman had thought as much. He had only offered for Mr. Bates's benefit. The chance to confess, the grateful moment of forgiveness—there must still be hundreds of opportunities before them, draped in every meeting like snakes in trees. Not now, then? No matter. Sprague was simple. Others, deeper in the upriver jungles, were more complex. Did Mr. Bates recognize a reference to the rogue geologist? An in-law, granted, at one time the hope of the family—now moribund, if not murdered; now swollen like a bloated pupa poisoned by its own inner organs, if not finally exploded. Had Mr. Bates heard nothing of this from his son? Was there no indication that this pivotal figure was dead? Wasn't that, when one came to it, precisely the question? No, *precisely* was hardly the correct word; *more or less* retained the flavor of the jungle better. But dead, dead was the question; or, a variation, as: if dead, noticeably so?

Such was the pure form of the investigation.

"But even that, Mr. Bates, even dead? Or rather, like the rest of us, strictly speaking, simply dying? Questions unanswered: the music of the police—unanswered and, as you will surely agree, unanswerable to those bogged in the mud. Thus, although the sense of the passage of time . . ."

"What can you possibly . . ."

"No! Agreed! Now is not the proper moment." The policeman spoke rapidly. His neck was cramping again. He kneaded both sides.

Unhappy socialists opposed the rogue geologist. They longed to control production, although their true calling

was in the simpler field of river piracy. So-called guerrillas before they lost their enthusiasm, they still retained
automatic weapons, limp uniforms, and an unpleasant
faith in slogans.

Mr. Bates would be wondering how his son stood in
relation to them. He could reassure himself that they
would hesitate to attack what they couldn't understand.
Their focus was on the workers, whose total lack of interest in any form of politics was considered to be the socialists' greatest stumbling block. It was reported they could
be spotted stalking along the crest of the slag heap,
muttering programs to each other and collaring any em-
ployee incautious enough to stray from the safety of the
furnaces.

The policeman rocked his head from side to side. The
spasm had been suppressed with difficulty. Did Mr. Bates
have any questions? No? Then they would resume their
patrol, if for no other reason than to instruct his men.
Searches expanded their outlook on life—a useful exercise,
if not allowed to drift past certain preset limits.

George Bates looked at the squad; beyond a kind of
repressed bewilderment, there was no longer any trace of
emotion on his face.

"They sleep badly," Detective Sergeant Xlong continued. "I hate their snoring, their groaning at nightmares,
their fear of the dark, the colorless sounds of their bones
beating against wet wood."

Nothing. If they disgusted Mr. Bates, he gave no indication. "At the veranda at one, then," the policeman concluded. Mr. Bates would be, as before, as always, a guest
of the police.

"And be careful returning. Probably the *naga* hasn't tasted your mother's milk."

George Bates did not point out that since Detective Sergeant Xlong himself had admitted the primitive charm made no difference, this parting remark was meaningless. Had he then accepted the nature of the contradiction? So the policeman believed, counting his silence as a clear chit toward compatibility.

Two soldiers were ordered to fall in behind the exhausted foreigner. Did Mr. Bates comfort himself with the idea that reasoning with the police was impossible? If so, then he must further conclude that he had little choice but to do what he was told. Things might work out very nicely. Detective Sergeant Xlong reminded himself that a willingness to form responses to patterns which on first contact appeared chaotic was one of the true flowers of the human condition.

"We're never better than when we trust each other," he mused aloud, but George Bates had already departed.

◄◊►◊◄◊►◊◄◊►◊◄◊►◊◄

"But, hey! Wait! George! It's not my fault! I'm just like you. You know, the innocent bystander that's getting . . ."

Mr. Bates pushed past Sprague and continued stalking down the alley. His forehead was swollen with angry red splotches. "Hang on a second!" Sprague limped after him, glancing around, obviously afraid of being in the open.

"We made a deal!"

Mr. Bates turned into a wider street which led to the central market square. Sprague scurried to catch up.

"Listen, George, in there they'll . . ."

"Get out of here!" said George Bates. "You're not getting any more money from me!"

"Money? But . . ."

Mr. Bates spotted a squad of soldiers standing at the corner of the market and turned toward them. Sprague hesitated, then dropped back out of sight.

Once in his room, George Bates stood beside his open window and picked at flakes of paint on the sill. Everything curled and cracked here; everything peeled and fell away at the slightest touch. He tore out a long sliver of wood and tossed it into the street below. The whole sill was rotten. He punched against the plaster wall. It was so soft and wet it oozed. He began to chip away damp chunks with his fingernails.

A gecko clinging head downward on the wall observed Mr. Bates. Its green lips curved into a smirk. Mr. Bates slapped at it but it darted up out of reach. There were moths, spiders, centipedes, all kinds of insects stuck on his ceiling. He snatched up his jacket and began slashing at them, sweeping some off onto the floor. He continued the attack until he was panting with frustration. Damaged insects lay quivering at his feet. A broken centipede dragged itself awkwardly as it made for the shelter of the bed. George Bates stepped on it; its shell cracked under his shoe.

He tossed his jacket onto the bed and stood in his open window again. Below him, partially concealed in the shadows of the nearest stall, a young woman was staring at his window. He'd never seen her before. She was dressed in the traditional sarong and sleeveless blouse of the upriver people, yet she seemed distinct from the other women in the market. When his eyes met hers, she looked away. He continued to watch her, and she raised her face again and accepted his gaze.

Mr. Bates picked her out when he reached the entrance of the hotel; but as he crossed toward her, she disappeared back into the crowded market square.

"You!" children shouted, never far from wherever he appeared. "Hello, you! Hello!"

Mr. Bates brushed past them. He began working his way through the nearby stalls. He went too far in one direction and hurried back, ignoring the complaints of shoppers as he struggled to get through them.

She wasn't at the near side. He searched the middle area again; she wasn't there either. He ran toward the food section, but it was too crowded. He would never be able to get through it. He moved along the edge helplessly until he reached the far end of the market, then turned back. She was standing right behind him, a puzzled expression on her face. She'd obviously been following him.

Mr. Bates stared at her. She became self-conscious and folded her arms over her breasts. Her face glistened with lines of sweat. George Bates didn't move. The young woman tilted her head up and looked at him, her lips lifting into a smile. Before Mr. Bates could do anything, she held out a long envelope.

"Is that a letter? From Philip?"

She nodded with quick jerks.

"Where is he?"

She seemed surprised by the question, but pointed vaguely toward the upriver jungle.

"Upriver?"

She nodded, and began to retreat down the alley. Mr. Bates came after her.

"Wait. I'm looking for him. I'm his father."

She stopped. "I know," she said. "That letter is for you."

"You can speak English?"

"No," she said. "Not well."

"How did you know I was his father?"

"Everybody knows."

"You can speak English, can't you? Listen, I want to ask you something."

"He knows you're here. He told me to give you this letter."

"Where is he?"

"He said you aren't supposed to worry."

"Where is he?"

"He said he had some business. He said you'd understand."

"Business?"

"I have to go. I have to go now."

"Take me with you. There's a cop, listen, there's a cop . . ."

"Cop?"

"A policeman, he's trying to . . ."

"I know," the young woman said, glancing at him curiously.

"You know him?"

She looked at George Bates as if she had expected him

to understand. "I'm Berthe," she added. "Berthe Xlong."

Mr. Bates repeated the name without apparently making anything of it.

"I'm his niece. Didn't Philip write to you?"

"Whose niece?"

"I thought he wrote. He wrote and wrote so I thought he wrote . . ."

"Yes, of course," George Bates said quickly. "I've had several letters."

"But he didn't write about . . ."

"Of course he did," George Bates interrupted. Her face had again clouded with confusion. Mr. Bates fumbled at the letter without opening it. She was waiting for him to say something, so he asked her to take him to his son. She shook her head. It was too dangerous.

"Dangerous?"

She looked down, her arms again folded over her chest.

"There's a crime," George Bates said. "Or there's going to be one. I know that sounds stupid like that; it sounds stupid to me, too."

"Stupid?"

"No, I mean, how he's going to be accused of something. As if there's no connection to anything, just—I don't know what. That cop, that policeman, your uncle? Really? He's the one that's going to . . ."

"Philip's innocent!" Berthe blurted out.

"Of course he is, but . . ."

She turned and hurried past him.

"Wait! What's going to happen?"

She paused at the corner and turned, her face once

again betraying confusion. George Bates stopped. He held his hands out toward her.

"What are you going to do?" she said in a small voice.

"Did Philip tell you to ask me that?"

"Why did you come?"

"To help him, of course."

"What are you going to do to help him?"

"What should I do?"

Berthe gave him a long, penetrating stare. For a moment she seemed to consider something; but at last she faltered. "Don't worry," she said and scampered down the alley.

He was left with the letter in his hand. He examined the back; the flap was sealed. There was no name, no address, just the blank surface of the paper, smudged with fingerprints.

"You!" Children had found him again. "You! Hello!"

George Bates passed between them, moving along the spine of the market square. He carried the letter without opening it, oblivious to the haggling voices all around him.

Detective Sergeant Xlong had agreed to take questions from his men. The jungle was a classroom, he explained. In the struggle against the rebels, certain techniques had been developed. They should understand there were lessons to be drawn from the forest. Had the monkeys become suddenly silent? Why? What meaning could be drawn from fresh slash marks on the trunks of certain trees? Was rubber being prepared? Was poison? Or was perhaps a guerrilla, frustrated by afternoons in the swamp, taking out his rage on nature? Ask questions. Observe the world, he urged them. It contained gifts to the wary.

His men were not to be shy; nor were they to slouch, for that matter. If they were too bashful to ask, didn't they run the risk of remaining ignorant forever? He would have them think of him in the role of their father-protector.

As senior officer and chief policy maker, he was aware of the value of education. Only the soldier who had received instruction could conceive of himself as replaceable. Education made civilization. The civilized man was he who knew the world could get along without him. Education, that was the future. Hadn't he himself been educated to within an inch of his life? They need only examine his face to see the resultant scars. Birth was painful; nothing came without a struggle. Getting beaten up was your body's way of letting you know you'd probably made a mistake. The same could be said for prolonged imprisonment, broken toes, gunshot wounds—all, all sure indications of error.

"Cholera, too," he added, "although, of course, the source is ambiguous. Still, with effort, blame could be attached."

They were to ask, he concluded. They were to trust him. He knew what was needed.

A militiaman stepped forward at last.

"Yes?"

The fellow looked at his feet.

"Yes?"

He said he spoke for the others. He said there was a question.

"Yes? Go on."

He hesitated.

"Yes?"

He said they wanted to know when they would be fed.

Detective Sergeant Xlong removed his police cap and studied the sweatband. He counted the stitches that joined the two ends. This was a hell of a life for a man, just a hell of a life.

George Bates wandered through the market clutching his unopened letter. He found himself among trays of jungle fruit spread oozing sugar to the sunlight and flies. He glanced behind him; the children were again occupied with their games, scratching in the mud with pointed sticks or wrapping each other with bits of vine. Mr. Bates slowed to examine a row of glass crocks filled with fermented pastes. A woman held out a taste on a chip of bamboo, but he refused it.

A dealer in fighting kites squatted surrounded by a group of boys, discussing problems of structure and design. George Bates stopped to watch; they immediately became silent. Mr. Bates moved on to study the wares of a dealer in herbal medicines. Beside him was a man hawking bloody joints from an animal he had killed. There was a curry merchant's shop, and Mr. Bates saw that the merchant, his wife, his children, even the dogs, were all tinted the bright yellow of their product.

Mr. Bates held up his letter. He picked at the flap with his finger, but didn't open it. A row of schoolgirls clutched each other, lined up waiting beside a soiled astrological curtain. Mr. Bates peered into the dark cave behind them.

An ancient woman began shrieking at him, her blind eyes twisted up staring into her forehead. He jerked back out; the girls laughed.

Mr. Bates jammed the letter into his pocket and turned toward the hotel.

Detective Sergeant Xlong divided his soldiers into squads. He tried to maintain an equivalent number of the less reliable in each group, but friends crossed to be with each other. Achieving anything resembling a balance required all his skill.

Once the ranks were formed, the junior officers were given their instructions. They were to act as pincers. They were to search the outskirts on their way back to town. If there were no further questions, they could depart at once.

One of the junior officers didn't join his group.

"Yes?"

The junior officers were discontented, he complained. This was not what they'd hoped.

"No?"

They didn't think it was fair.

"No," Detective Sergeant Xlong agreed, well aware of what they wanted. "But there's no danger here. It's only Sprague."

The junior officer kicked at a lump of mud stubbornly. It was a small thing, a few rounds each, to make them feel fierce.

Detective Sergeant Xlong sent them on their way. He didn't want to be unkind, but they were less likely to injure themselves with empty rifles. They had to appreciate that it was the fact that they operated as a group which mattered—the many unquestioningly obeying the word of the one, *that* was the police. Discipline was more important than ferocity. They had to learn to button each tunic button in order. They had to understand they all must do it in exactly the same manner. Fear, he told himself, was—technically speaking—fine, as far as it went. But in today's jungle, what was wanted was organization; the crowding called for it; the weather shouted for its salve. The solution was cocked in the counting. You, and then you, and then you—A, B, C: neatness, predictability, perfection—it was enough to make him squeeze himself with pleasure.

Here one could always return to teeth: the fellow stuffed into a wet stump, white arm dangling out of the branches; night howls, drums with sudden silence, curdled milk—one knew what one knew.

Besides, he smiled, they would have their afternoon with real bullets soon enough. He knew what was best.

Mr. Bates's hands hung loosely before him. He didn't look at his fingers. The two sheets of notepaper twitched between his feet like severed wings.

He stood and crossed to the window. There was no one in the market watching for him. Down the alley, a knot of boys fought over a bent bicycle wheel. Spokes broke free with muffled twangs, lacerating the bloody fingers that snatched at them.

George Bates returned to the market square. In the central stall, a merchant had a row of young sea turtles lined up on their backs to die. A sunburned flipper would occasionally trace through the gesture of swimming, although hopelessly, awkwardly, as if imperfectly remembering.

105

Their beaks gasped open with deep sucks of air, and as Mr. Bates watched, their eyelids blinked tears pink with blood down the bony plates of their faces.

Mr. Bates's fingers curled into the flesh of his palms. There had been nothing in the letter. Beyond recognizing that he had come, Philip had made no connections. It could as easily have been sent to a father safe in Los Angeles. There was no reference to any problem. The tone was that of a tourist enjoying his travels.

The merchant's little daughter splashed water from a bucket down the row of turtles, although neglecting the ones nearest Mr. Bates. "Wait," he croaked, but she scurried timidly back into the shadows of her father's shop.

Heat radiated from the turtles' shells. George Bates sagged to the ground at the end of the row. Clouds blew into the glazed Mesozoic eye of the turtle nearest him, clouds piling up from a distant sunlit sea and thickening with the creature's death.

George Bates held his head in his hands. Some turtles still swam against the humid air. The little girl was hovering with a bucket of water again, afraid to come any closer to the old man.

❖❰❖❰❖❰❖❰❖❰❖❰❖❰❖❰

"Berthe Xlong?"

"Anything you could tell me at all," said Mr. Bates. "It's very important that I see her."

"There's no Berthe Xlong registered here."

"I know. I told you she wasn't a guest at the hotel. But I thought you might have some idea where I could find her."

"Who?"

"Berthe Xlong."

The desk clerk turned the registry toward Mr. Bates. The ink of the signatures had blurred so badly it was impossible to read most of the names. "You see? No Berthe Xlong here."

George Bates waited in the hotel doorway until a pack of children had drifted past.

He crossed through the market square with his hands jammed in his pockets. In the back corner he found the blind fortune-teller. The schoolgirls were gone; the old woman crouched beside her canvas awning, dipping the hem of her skirt into a cup of gray liquid and working at the rims of her dead white eyes. A shopkeeper next to her spotted George Bates and bent to whisper into the old woman's ear.

"You!" the fortune-teller shrieked. "Stay away! Stay away from me!"

"You speak English? Listen, I . . ."

"Stay away!"

"I need some help. My son's lost. He's in trouble."

"Stay away from me!" The old woman thrust herself backward, wrenching out a rope that supported her awning.

"But I won't hurt you."

"No! Stay away!" She covered her eye sockets with the palms of her hands as if to protect them from attack.

George Bates tried to explain that there had been a young woman with him. She'd brought a message. He had to find her again.

The woman who had alerted the fortune-teller yelled

something to her neighbor on the other side, and both broke into shouts of laughter. A man with a machete suddenly jumped into the alley, silencing them with a short bark.

Mr. Bates started to turn away as the uproar spread to the next section of the market. People came running from both directions. Another angry man joined the first and they stood together staring at him. George Bates saw that the second man cradled a rock in one hand.

"Listen, do you speak English?"

"Hello!" Some boys darted in from the side. "You!"

Mr. Bates glanced again at the old woman. She was partially hidden behind the collapsed rear wall of her awning. "I'm . . ." he began, but stopped. All fear was gone from her face. She had settled into a trance. Her eyes were again rolled back up, staring into her forehead. Mr. Bates saw she was smiling at him, almost coquettishly. It was like an invitation, a seduction.

He retreated involuntarily, his hand reaching behind him for support. He felt the flat blade of a machete drawn up the backs of his legs. The man with the machete was also smiling. His face, too, contained the hint of an offer.

Mr. Bates broke through the crowd clogging the alley. "You!" children shouted after him. "Hello! Hello!"

He could hear their laughter all the way to the edge of the market square.

"Knuckles, knots, nuts." The policeman repeated each word twice, then returned the day's lesson to his shirt pocket. Spelling, pronunciation—there was a wonder to the word. Grammar was like love—whatever that was; both made you want to line somebody up and search him.

He knew he could become whatever he could say, but beyond that? A blank. Nothing but jungle, the predictable effects of moisture, and the past.

"That past," he said aloud to himself. His neck hurt. His pants were wet; his shirt was wet; sweat coated his face. He thought of his squads encircling the town. He slapped his palms against his face, splattering out a warm spray. Rainbows, juices, which underpants would Moule be wearing? Pink? Mauve? Banana? Taupe? Tangerine? He'd listed them once, spent a secret morning with her bureau drawers. That had been a wonderful day. He'd walked through the world with the words in his pocket, steadily erupting from an inner glow. Was that love? He'd wondered at the time. A catalogue? There was something to the idea; and as it had grown within him, swelling his consciousness, it was all he could do to restrain himself from rushing back at once with a fresh note pad and pawing through her brassieres.

He stood, his shoulders were stiff; his spine seemed to be calcifying. He had no choice but to return and place himself in Moule's hands. Moule, he thought, smiling. He really would have to ask himself some hard questions about her one of these days.

George Bates passed through a series of alleys until he discovered the grove of trees hung with limp strips of white paper, swollen now from the last rain and puffy as dead fingers. He paused at the nearest of these and reached out; but instead of plucking one down, he hesitated for a moment, then hurried past.

He pushed at the door of the cockpit without results. It now seemed to be bolted. There was no keyhole, no

109

doorknob, only a crude wooden handle. The door might be barred on the inside. He tugged at the handle; it tore off easily. The screws were nothing but rough stumps, so badly had they been eaten with rust.

There was no one in the alley. Mr. Bates pressed tentatively against the door. Perhaps it was stuck, bloated with moisture. He leaned more heavily against it. The door broke loose and collapsed into the cockpit with a sodden crash. Mr. Bates sprawled on top of it. He glanced outside; the alley was still empty. He tried to fit the door into its hole, but it fell back in his arms. He finally pulled strips of bamboo from a broken cock basket and used those to wedge it shut.

He held his hands over his nose. The stench inside the gloomy cockpit was as oppressive as it had been the day before.

His eyes adjusted to the dim light. The mud of the cockpit floor curved in a smooth slope up into the mud of the walls, as if the whole room had been hollowed out of a single lump of clay.

A section of rooms opened off from the far side of the ring. Mr. Bates quietly crossed to the first of these. The inside was dark; he didn't go in. Electric wires were looped along the ceiling; but as in the main arena, all the overhead lights had been smashed.

"Sprague?" he called softly into the blackness. "Where are you?"

He held his breath. There was no reply.

Mr. Bates followed along the wall to the next room. The greasy plaster yielded to the pressure of his fingertips, as resilient as the belly of a frog. He reached for a light switch, running his hand all around the inside of the door-jamb but finding nothing.

"Sprague?" Nothing. There was no reply.

Detective Sergeant Xlong didn't knock. He knew the door would be open. Moule was sitting in her chair beside the shuttered window. A single wedge of light fell across her lower body. She didn't look around when she heard him come in. His fingers were cramped; he had trouble manipulating his buttons. He could see the thick flesh of her left thigh, exposed from the knee to the top of the hip.

"Moule?" he said in a civilian voice. "Are you getting ready?"

Her knee flexed; her calf and foot unfolded into the light filtering between two sections of her bamboo blind. She had fastened a small gold chain to her left ankle.

"Moule?"

The other leg lifted into the light, parallel to the first. He saw a flash of color; her arms had come into view. Her fingers were short and blunt; the underpants hung from them, a curved web capturing the light like a smile at mealtime.

"Slowly, slowly."

She spread the nylon loops wider. First the left foot, then the right surfaced from the darkness and was inserted into the elastic circlets of the leg bands.

The policeman felt his heart fill with emotion. "Moule," he said. Was love then a muscle spasm? A kind of palsy, perhaps? Focused from the unaired quarters of the imagination? "Moule," he said, "Moule." Was passion motor responses maintained at a functional level? Hard questions for a moment of romance; tough questions anytime.

Moule arched her back, lifting her thighs higher and forcing her lower belly into the light as she drew the underpants up her legs and fitted them skillfully into place.

Banana, then, the policeman recognized immediately; it was to be banana today. Good, that was good. He too had been feeling distinctly banana.

"Moule," he said, and watched her hand search the floor for her brassiere.

George Bates reached the end of the hall. The entire area was clogged with rubble, mostly smashed spectators' bleachers that looked as if they might have been broken intentionally. Mr. Bates started to return up the other side of the hall when he noticed that the rubble had been arranged in such a way as to allow a narrow passage—no wider than a man's legs, but carefully opened all the way to the back wall. He followed this; it led to a staircase going down, also packed with crushed benches and broken cock baskets.

George Bates descended the stairs as silently as possible. The basement was suffused with a soft green glow, like the underwater illumination of a swimming pool at night. He reached the bottom; there was nothing to see other than more smashed benches. It seemed impossible that the cock ring could have held so many spectators.

The basement had once been floored, although the broken planks appeared to be much older than those of the stairs. Most of the junk at the bottom of the pile had so thoroughly decomposed and was so overgrown with mosses that there was no longer a clear distinction between where the remains ended and the mud began. The ceiling, supported by thick timbers, was composed of black clay. It was like being in a mine shaft, or a grave.

The rubble formed a sequential flow of generation upon generation of spectators' benches, each serving an allotted term before joining its ancestors in the basement. Mr. Bates bent to scratch at the black earth beneath his feet and came up with a rich humus—a pulp that had once been wood, bamboo, feathers, bones, blood.

Mr. Bates had never been so subterranean. It was as if he had descended to where dead matter crossed back into being alive. He crouched down again and placed both palms against the decaying humus. The soil was living. He could see the lightless eyes of fungi that thrived there like nodes growing upon the logs of corpses.

He stood up. He turned toward the stairs, then stopped. Caught in the green light against the far wall, Sprague hung suspended from wires taut as guitar strings. Stripped to the waist, every bone in his back etched with shadows, he was patiently attempting to teach his cock how to fight.

George Bates couldn't have uttered a sound. The bird stood stupidly in the rotted duff, its red eyes blinking as the twisted cock handler held his skinny arms out like wings, craned back his neck, the wires straining with the weight of his body, and painfully forced his dead leg up in the air high enough to model the act of spurring downward—all the while whispering, "Chain Saw," cooing at the bird, "Chain Saw, Chain Saw," and demonstrating again what he wanted.

Mr. Bates made it up the stairs with almost no noise; but in the darkness of the hall, he blundered into walls, crashed through piles of rubble, and at last fell sprawling

113

into the main heap of cock baskets filling the far corner of the pit.

He tore at the door to the outside alley. He had forgotten that the hinges were gone. The whole thing fell in on top of him, cracking his forehead and splitting in half. He thrust away the two rotten slabs of door, and, struggling to his knees, crawled into the alley.

He panted, his head hanging down, sucking in huge gulps of fresh air. He glanced up and saw boots. Soldiers stood in front of him, as surprised to see him as he was to see them. He looked down the alley; there were more soldiers, a lot more. He was surrounded, and so was Sprague.

Mr. Bates got to his feet and brushed off his clothes. A junior officer placed a hand on his forearm but he jerked it away. The man didn't insist.

❖❙(❖❙(❖❙(❖❙(❖❙(❖❙(❖❙(

"I can come back. I didn't . . ."

The soldiers blocked the door. Detective Sergeant Xlong motioned George Bates into the room without lifting his face from the table. Moule's hands hesitated for a moment, then continued kneading, as yet unable to loosen his shoulders.

"I can wait outside. I thought you said lunch."

He had said lunch. Lunch was next. Without the application of his little friend's fingers, he would be too tight to swallow. He simply chose not to tempt choking.

He told Moule to get a bullet and give it to the soldiers who had brought George Bates. He knew they would rush back to the barracks with their prize and probably blow a hole through the wall, if not through one of their fellows; but initiative should occasionally be rewarded. Besides, they were due for a touch of reinforcement to help them get over their growing sullenness.

George Bates started to follow the soldiers back out the open door.

"Haven't you ever seen a woman in her underwear?"

"Yes, but not quite so . . . she . . ."

"It's the weather," Detective Sergeant Xlong said.

"You can sit here," Moule added. Mr. Bates should try to relax. She was used to people looking at her.

"Oh."

George Bates sat down; the policeman closed his eyes. Moule climbed up to straddle him, paused to flex her powerful fingers, then buried her thumbs in the chuck muscle below his neck.

All three held their silence. The only sound was the slap and suck of Moule's palms as she pried at the swollen ropes of the policeman's upper body. Once the tension was drained from his neck, the remaining quarters would respond.

"I want to make a compromise," George Bates blurted out, no doubt uncomfortable with the wet mounds of flesh before him. The policeman smiled without opening his eyes, his face calm as a fresh grenade.

"I've decided you're right. We should work together. I'm willing to forget what's happened and start again."

115

Detective Sergeant Xlong shifted one arm so that it hung from the table. Did the foreigner expect him to seize this offer like a grateful child? He knew complicity was what was required, yet he hesitated.

"But you don't understand my son. He has problems, but he wouldn't do anything illegal. He's innocent, and so is . . ."

"Sprague?"

"It's not the same, but . . ."

"We're all innocent until proven guilty."

"That's the same as the American . . ."

"In this case, I speak metaphorically," the policeman interrupted somewhat more sharply. He was becoming annoyed by George Bates's tone.

He remembered how his elder brother's innocence had led him to his death. He was only a child on the day his brother had been killed, yet that moment continued to ride inside him, insistent as a chip of shrapnel lodged against a bone.

George Bates began a tedious explanation of his son's emotional history. Detective Sergeant Xlong continued to think only of his brother. Their kampong had been upriver from a new settlement American missionaries had established on the coast. The three Xlong brothers were allowed to attend the school on the mud flats. They floated their dugout canoe downriver with the morning flood. After their lessons, they tied up behind the river packet to be towed home. They became the pride of their kampong, as well as the seeds of its destruction.

George Bates droned on about a series of therapists. Moule's professional curiosity became aroused; she asked questions. Mr. Bates turned his conversation toward her, more at ease with her near-nudity. In Hong Kong, too, she told him, youths were troubled.

The policeman remembered how out of place swamp stains had seemed in the classroom. At school he and his brothers were seated on a bench and each given a book and a pen and a piece of heavy paper. They were introduced to the pleasures to be found in the Psalms. They were issued pants and taught how to wear them. Here, they were told, one was careful to conceal one's genitals—a principle his elder brother, in a moment of masculine bravado brought on by the presence of Cynthia, the headmaster's beautiful teenage daughter, had violated. He did capture her attention, however—an act that was to cost him his life.

"Our schools have developed special programs." Mr. Bates explained that a variety of creativity-encouraging situations were provided for the students. They were taught to express themselves, although this often produced no more than a recounting of the previous night's television programs.

Moule nodded; she leaned back for a moment to rest her hands. Mr. Bates had evidently accustomed himself to the squeak of wet flesh on the table. Detective Sergeant Xlong suspected that George Bates took comfort in the net of Moule's underpants. He wondered if there wasn't something of the police in Mr. Bates, a touch of that fundamental shyness by which even incipient members of the force recognized each other.

"I too have been taught," the detective sergeant said. "I liked English grammar. Did your son study it?"

117

"Not exactly; there was something in communication skills, and a lot of unstructured video poetry . . ."

"I liked grammar rules. I was elected classroom monitor every term I was in attendance. This was by acclamation. I stood for office unopposed."

"Singing," Moule exclaimed, standing to walk down the policeman's spine, "and dancing!"

George Bates was silenced by the sight of her erect body.

Education, thought the policeman, grunting with pleasure. His timid younger brother had been skilled at art, while his elder brother was a champion at any sport played within sight of the headmaster's house. Their days were filled with history, arithmetic, reading, and music— always served with cautionary references from the Bible. Detective Sergeant Xlong had learned to enjoy the Good Book, with its prophets and punishments, its hooked martyrs suspended by their heels, all the joys and violations of the religious life.

He would have liked to explain to George Bates how he had been tempted by the call of the cloth but in the end had determined that it didn't have the immediate impact of the police.

He felt happier. His little friend climbed down from the table and stood in front of George Bates. She rested her hands on her hips and asked if he would like a liqueur.

Mr. Bates shook his head. He had difficulty lifting his eyes above her knees. Detective Sergeant Xlong, in a gesture of affection and reconciliation, raised one steady finger and smoothed out the damp nylon triangle bunched up in the cleft between her buttocks.

"Ask him if he wants a whiskey," he suggested.

George Bates glanced at the policeman and refused.

"Our orderly days in the classroom confused my brothers and me, Mr. Bates; for at night we went back to the long-house, back to the filed teeth and scarred bodies of our tribe, trying to solve equations or memorize verse while warriors drunk on rice beer howled mournfully at the moon.

"What do you imagine we were supposed to make of ourselves?"

"What?"

He had continued to watch Moule. She now stood before the open window, catching the air and wiping her legs with a wet towel.

"Never mind," the policeman said with an edge to his voice. "You don't have to tell me now.

"My legs," he called; "if you've rested."

George Bates suddenly asked him to name a price, to set a condition, some form to file, anything.

"In order to make up for the past?"

"I just want to get out of here!"

"I'd thought you were becoming more at home with us."

"Listen, whatever you want."

"Are you offering a bribe to a policeman?"

"What do you want?"

Moule applied her full strength to the detective ser-geant's thighs. She could sense the anger welling up inside him.

"What were we to them?" the policeman demanded. "Why did they teach us?"

"Who?" George Bates asked.

Detective Sergeant Xlong's lips felt for stanzas he had once been forced to memorize. " 'The curfew tolls the knell of parting day,' " he said in a bitter voice, forcing a smile as Moule struggled against the constrictions in his legs. "And, 'The lowing herd wind o'er the lea,' and, 'And leaves the world . . .' No, you see? And, 'The plowman homeward plows his weary way,' then, 'And leaves the world to darkness and to me,' and, 'Now fades . . . Now fades . . .' I forget what fades."

His legs were numb; they would soon be cramped.

"A 'lea,' " he exclaimed, his voice cracking. "What's that? A 'knell,' a 'tolls,' a 'lowing herd.' What's that to us? What kind of thing is it to make us know that?"

George Bates's face was blank. Moule recognized the nature of the crisis and climbed up onto the policeman's back. Clutching him powerfully between her thighs, she began beating at the base of his neck with piston strokes.

Mr. Bates asked the policeman if he knew what it meant. No, he groaned. It was poetry. They were only taught to remember it.

"It has a kind of sense to it, you know."

"You like 'leas'?"

"No, but the meaning . . ."

"Do you think that was expected of us!" The policeman reared up and slapped his palm against the table, beating time. " 'The,' " *slap*, " 'lowing,' " *slap*, " 'herd,' " *slap!*

Moule tried to ease him back down onto the table.

"We were savages!" he shouted. "Nobody expected us to know anything! They told us to line up! I learned that well!" His voice dropped to a snarl. "I line up well and I line others up well, too."

"Easy," Moule whispered, "breathe deeply."

"Put a person," he continued, "against that wall," pointing with his fist, "and I'll line him up!"

"Don't!" Moule pleaded.

"It is," he gasped, his body locking shut, "a fundamental duty—duty of the police to—to determine places—places for things, and things—things for places!" His face slapped flat against the wood with a wet smack.

"Listen." Moule turned to Mr. Bates. "Maybe you better go now."

"No!" the policeman insisted, straining to raise his head. "Cynthia . . ." He halted, paralyzed by the onset of a neck cramp. He held himself still. He had only a few seconds left. "Can you tell me why—why you send us your—your—your damaged children? Do you think you—you are—exposing them to—to—to die?"

George Bates's chair scraped back as he stood, his face drained of all color. The policeman's neck twisted up against its vise, stretching to meet the confrontation. They glared at each other, one frozen, the other trembling with rage. Detective Sergeant Xlong slowed his breathing. He reminded himself that he was a policeman. He reminded himself that indignation was categorized under: "Responses comma Emotional," and that this referred to displays unacceptable in public situations, and that all situations—save the few moments of solitude one seized in one's police hammock—were relentlessly public.

George Bates declared that he would not submit to this abuse. He had been dragged here against his will. Nevertheless, he had made efforts. He had shown good faith. But no more!

Detective Sergeant Xlong would have acted had he not so lost control of himself. Moule strained with the effort, but she could no longer even manage to hold her own against the cramping muscles. One section of his body after another locked itself against him. Without his masseuse, he would long since have been strangled like a rabbit caught in the coils of a python.

"You're nothing but a bully!"

"No," Moule insisted. "Leave, leave now!"

George Bates stood quivering with confusion. The policeman's hips locked; his knees locked. "Mr. Bates," he began, but his little friend pressed herself against his back and whispered in his ear that he must protect himself. She couldn't save him.

Moule jumped down off the table. She grabbed a kimono and dragged the foreigner out of the room.

"Lunch!" the policeman croaked at their backs, squeezing himself against the attack.

"He'll be there!" Moule said and slammed the door.

His ankles locked; his toes stiffened, spreading out; he was totally immobilized.

He could sweat; he could salivate, weep, pass urine—liquids would leave him; but beyond that, he was reduced to furniture—a heap, a low hill, a simple landscape hunched under the weather.

He thought of how his elder brother had been distracted from the moment he first caught sight of the headmaster's beautiful teenage daughter. He had never had any skill at lining up; and from that time, he was like a fellow too full of fermented cassava gruel. He had had nothing to compare her to. She had held out a world of mystery none of them could do any more than wonder at.

The policeman had believed in Cynthia as much as his elder brother had, and sometimes his survival struck him as being an oversight—one due at any moment to be rectified.

Gradually he felt the attack begin to pass. As the tingling returned to his legs, he dragged himself to his little friend's liqueur bottle. He saw his uniform heaped on her bed, but he had no strength to dress himself. He gazed at his groin; there was never any visible damage. He sagged his belly. He felt lonely. Life was like waiting for your name to be called.

He sank down at the foot of the bed and returned his attention to his breathing.

He had suspected he might have to pay, but not quite so severely. Truly, emotion was the chief flaw in members of the police.

◆❮◆❮◆❮◆❮◆❮◆❮◆❮◆❮◆❮

"Maudlin? Me?"

Moule was down on her hands and knees, peering under the love seat, reaching in to sort through the objects he had hidden there. She had managed to track down everything but a single elusive boot.

"Teach us to be objective!" He groaned and raised his eyes to the maps of moisture on the ceiling. "My ancestors were cannibals; how do you think that makes me feel?"

Moule no doubt knew she wouldn't be required to comment. He watched her forlornly, his face still swollen.

Self-consciousness with menus, fear of the comments of waiters, the equilibrium upset by the sight of a dining fork, these were the hurdles they had shared.

She stood with her hands on her hips and studied the disarray. She didn't bother to ask for help; he would only stir the room further with his floundering. Moule often complained that since he had begun visiting her, it was all she could do to maintain her possessions in the same locations for two days in a row.

The detective sergeant hung his head. He searched compulsively. He needed to be felt by the world. It was the static nature of objects that starved him, that drove him to empty drawers, to carry things from one spot to another, to tip over furniture, to remove pictures from their frames, and to tuck the frames themselves in with dishes. It was loneliness, he had once remarked, that drove him to pack cups under the bed—anything, any action that would leave the world altered, that would thus establish the difference between himself and, say, a jar of chutney.

"Chutney?"

"You've never felt that way?"

Moule had shaken her head. Sometimes his problems extended beyond her comprehension.

Detective Sergeant Xlong leaned his face against the velvet Moule had glued to her walls. He was tempted to pluck at a moist flap which had puffed loose from the seam, but he snatched up his cap instead. The insignia above the bill seemed suddenly futile.

"All my life I've been ashamed!"

"You're too sensitive," Moule said from the other room, then gave a cry. The boot had been found.

The policeman shook his head, his cap crushed in one fist. Life was no garden. The greasy slope of wet earth above his elder brother's grave hung over him again; and he, a child, crept out of the brush and stood aghast at the foot of that slippery mound of red clay. He recalled the shape of his little brother, cocked like a bow and clenching himself in silent rage—the perfected self-denial found first in those resolved to be protectors of the dead. And again he saw his brother's bitter charge, felt the slashing attack as his little brother's pointed stick drove him from the grave; and again, he understood the word remorse.

The policeman knew at that moment that his brother would die, that he himself would die; and, with a rueful touch of relief, wondered briefly if it—death—might not have already happened without his noticing—freeing him thus from, if nothing else, lunch.

"Put on your shirt, Bobo; put on your police pants. They always make you feel better."

He sighed. It was hard to drain much satisfaction from the fantasy of one's death. Would Moule mourn him? Would she regret all the times she'd failed to do what he wanted? Yearn to live those moments again? But she always did what he wanted, he reminded himself; the problem was coming up with sufficient wants to keep her occupied.

What should he do? Didn't he have to choose? He could consult his police handbook, but it was double-edged; every assertion was coupled with an immediate and equivalent denial.

Did that mean there wasn't value? Did that disallow right and wrong? No, he affirmed, there was wrong; life

125

would be unpoliceable without it. There was wrong, wrong, wrong—it rang like a bell.

He picked up a small porcelain ballerina and recalled the joy he had once received from inserting the little dancer's pointed foot into the vulnerable open leaves of a head of Chinese cabbage. Such were the pleasures of his works and days. He grasped the figurine by the head and foot. It would be a simple matter to snap the leg off.

Moule stood in the doorway observing him, patiently drawing a wet towel over her belly. He replaced the figurine on its pedestal. There was wrong, then, but from that could one postulate right? Here was a problem. He studied the unchanging face of the tiny dancer. Why would anyone want such a thing? He had no clue. It was Moule's; did that mean she liked it?

He concluded it would never do to damage it. He settled for turning its face toward the wall—proof, he suspected, that in him, at least, self-denial was far from perfected.

He stood; she would hand him his clothing. It occurred to him that perhaps she understood him better than he realized. He wondered if he should ask her something, inquire about her history, what she liked, her last name, perhaps? Something in the area of her family? Something to indicate he was interested in her?

He focused his eyes. Beyond being able to identify one, he had very little skill at beginnings; thus he tended to ignore them. The forms of events—other than those codified in the police philosophy—were like objects in sacks; he recognized outlines without ever seeing what was inside. He squinted, wondering if what she might like was a kiss. Moule was a mystery. He reached up to pluck tentatively at the rubbery leather of his lower lip. Would she enjoy him rubbing it against her cheek? Her ear? How would that feel? He had no idea. Sensation dropped away from his fingertips like birds shot out of the sky. No, he really didn't feel he had much understanding of openings.

Could there nevertheless be said to be a detectable moral order governing the universe? He considered his official underpants held out toward him, gray and heavy as rain, the design determined by those who would never wear them—which perhaps accounted for the coarseness of the web and the excessive number of buttons.

He stepped into them firmly. His leg muscles functioned. He was a policeman; he could feel it again for the first time since his spasms.

Could one then detail the possibilities of doing to others what they did to you? Could one moreover morally try to get in the first shot? Ethical considerations, he had learned, ought if possible to be grounded in metaphysics. Moule wrinkled her nose and held his undershirt out at arm's length. He should have had it washed the day before. He couldn't remember if he had a clean one, but it seemed unlikely. And metaphysics, in turn, could be stuffed into logic; and logic battered back into mathematics; and that, he concluded, comforted, was just counting, the fingers folded one by one into the formation of a fist—for him, home.

He relied on being forgiven, he knew. This was what loosened him enough to allow scope for action, to risk error. But then shouldn't he too attempt to forgive? Obviously, he should. He knew that. Moule held out his heavy khaki pants—pants he had come to depend on more than any other single thing—pants that late at night in the privacy of his police office he occasionally addressed comments toward in familiar terms, actually took into his confidence and confessed his secret fears to—and pants from which, in turn, he felt he derived a certain amount of understanding, of warmth perhaps, if not actual affection. Love was sticky, he knew. One would do well not to ask too much of one's garments.

Moule handed him his police shirt. Here were insignias, pressed out of chips of tin and sewn on like little knives. He felt better. A saber, a star, crossed rifles over the national symbol: a cobra—knotted and, from the look on its face, apparently coughing. The bits of tin had become discolored by sweat and his morning in the swamp. He burnished them against his sleeve.

He placed his police cap firmly on his head. He tilted the bill down to shade his eyes, erasing Moule's body from the waist up and thus facilitating a moment alone with her round belly—the flesh as golden as the insides of a split mango; her underpants, more a gesture of demarcation than anything the laws of modesty might suggest, joined the two smooth thighs with the equally smooth belly—three distinct shapes, he thought, counting.

Someday he certainly would have to ask himself some very serious questions about what he made of such things.

She held out his pistol belt; the leather was slick with moisture. This was a good world, he mused, examining the holster for patches of rot; one could live here. He buckled the pistol belt firmly to his waist. He was ready.

Moule held the door open. It seemed there was something he should say to her. He ran his tongue behind his teeth. He could smell the street below, waiting for him.

"How do I look?" he asked.

❖❰❈❰❈❖❰❈❰❈❖❰❈❰❈❖❰❈❰❈❖❰❈

"Fing!"

"Fing?"

"Fing was his name. He was tall and handsome and lusty. He could crack buffalo bones between his molars to suck the marrow. He had a knife scar on his shoulder and an arrow hole in his foot. He could curl up the sides of his tongue and wiggle his ears. He could tell fine, long stories—mostly lies, of course, the exaggerations being what we younger boys enjoyed.

"Fing could run faster, spit seeds farther, and throw rocks more accurately than anyone else in the kampong. He was a sure future candidate for headman.

"His murder shadows me like a dog, Mr. Bates. This is why I have taken an interest in your case."

The waiter returned with a bucket full of rags. He wiped up the mess Detective Sergeant Xlong had spilled on the floor of the veranda. Smashed bits of canapés were everywhere.

"A personal interest, that is, as well as a professional one. Like my brother, I have difficulty in avoiding what I cannot understand. Why you are here is clear. Why your son came here is not. Cynthia, too, puzzled me. Fing became convinced he was at his best on his knees. They prayed for hours in an attempt to clean out his soul. Why did she care? Was it because so many women had rolled

129

under the pump of his coupling? Was it that, young as he was, the butt of his kris had already achieved several tufts of human hair—evidence of his participation in raids that had resulted in successful kills? What did she want from him? Why did she and her father come so far, pass through so many trials, all so that they could hold the mirror up to my brother and teach him to see himself as they saw him?

"Why would anyone do such a thing?"

Mr. Bates's plate of hors d'oeuvres sat before him untouched. He didn't ask what the policeman's confession had to do with his son.

"Perhaps we younger boys couldn't appreciate the headmaster's daughter, but we were as obsessed with her as Fing was. We asked him what he did down on his knees, and he said he didn't do anything. 'Why didn't you?' we asked. He said because he didn't know what he was supposed to do. 'Then why do you do it?' we said. He'd just drift away.

"All we knew about kneeling was that from behind you could see Cynthia wore wonderful petticoats under her skirts. We stole one of these and carried it back to study. It was musty and tasted of dried sweat. We could make no progress with it and at last asked Fing what it meant. He had never noticed one before. When we told him where we got it, he became filled with rage and confusion. We younger boys were forced to flee into the jungle.

"Our confidence in him was badly shaken."

The policeman fitted one hand around a fresh glass of whiskey. He was sorry Moule wasn't there to see how calmly he was conversing with the foreigner. He felt a twinge of tenderness for her without allowing himself the leisure to pursue it.

"Can you appreciate that I was a child? You don't have a good understanding of the police, Mr. Bates. Do you think we don't feel pain? Our duty demands we proceed in an orderly manner; but inside, we bleed."

"I'm sure you do, Detective Sergeant. Nevertheless . . ."

"No," the policeman said sharply. "Don't tell me. Perhaps you believe I couldn't accept Cynthia, and you may be right. The need to investigate forces us into odd postures; we can rarely relax. This terrible strain feeds our loneliness. We come to our crimes hungry for a touch of human warmth. But the citizens we are sworn to protect conceal information. We are like doctors. 'Where does it hurt?' we ask, and the fellow with the broken leg points slyly to his elbow."

"Yes, well, I can see . . ."

"Can you? Is it so much to request? An occasional kind word to the officer snarled in such a poorly organized situation. There are so many loose ends one would be better off without. Can you understand that?"

"Well, yes, I suppose, but . . ."

"It is the chief frustration of the police to be unable to determine what we want. Amputate! we shout in our hearts. Stop the gangrene short of the groin!

"Here, Mr. Bates, I speak in figures.

"Short of the groin! As I said, in our hearts we shout, but the fool fights for his legs and is dead within the space of a day. The weather, as I have indicated before, is also to blame.

"Do you follow me, Mr. Bates?"

"Well, that last part, I don't quite . . ."

"An example is the death of my brother. There were indications from the beginning but no way to make sense of them. Cynthia was concerned with the question of copulation. She said she wanted them to be pure. Why? we younger boys asked, but he ignored us. He said she seized him by the wrists and whispered that he should never again roll with women. Why not? we wondered. He said she made him swear not to touch any woman. We were as puzzled by this as he was. He said it was the only thing he could give her; so he gave it. None of us had any advice. We told him we wished such things wouldn't happen. He made no reply.

"One day he took me down the riverbank. I trailed my pointed stick as I listened to him attempt to explain what was happening. She said she wanted him to appreciate things that enriched one's life. She showed him photographs of famous places in America. He told how he stared hard at each example. He knew he had gotten off to a slow start. Cynthia would teach him how to be polite. He told of the tremendous number of choices she could distinguish—how to stand, how to sit, how to hold a cup. As he learned how many ways there were to make a mistake, he began to grow cautious. At the end of a session, he would walk away politely for a hundred meters, then bolt through the forest, working off his pent-up confusion on anything that crossed his path.

"Can you understand we were children, Mr. Bates? We had no weapons to save him. He had accepted the judgments of her culture. He sat up at night by himself on the porch of our longhouse and stared at the jungle. He made no move to enjoy anything. Do you think we couldn't understand the danger? Fing was our best, yet he seemed to have no chance against the young foreign woman's amazing power to make distinctions.

"Once he sat on a flat rock with his feet on the ground and his knees together. 'How do I look?' he asked me. I said he looked fine. Then he pulled one knee up and crossed it over the other. 'How do I look now?' I was puzzled, but I thought he looked all right. Then he pulled his upper leg up under his chest and the other up next to it until both knees were under his chin. He asked me how he looked and when I failed to answer, he threw himself off the rock, crying that one of the three was wrong, and strode hopelessly into the jungle.

"Can you tell me why you are the ones who decide such questions?

"My brother was not a fool. Perhaps each time he gave in to her he thought it would be the last. His failure was that he had no plan, nothing to set up against her concern, no set of rules to wrap around his knuckles, and so no way to defend himself against each successive step."

The sky closed over with afternoon rain clouds. Waiters hurried to pull the front tables back from the edge of the veranda.

"Rules, Mr. Bates, stiff rules, rules gripped in the solitary fist . . ." The policeman held up his hand. He had only 80 percent articulation in his fingers. "You will find I am not the simple victim my brother was."

Detective Sergeant Xlong looked at his glass. The temperature had dropped slightly before the approaching rain; insects paused in their shrill screaming. The policeman scratched at his elbow. His fingernails filled with crushed egg, causing him to reflect on how easily things spilled here.

"What do you want from me?" Mr. Bates asked, evidently uncomfortable in the sudden silence. "I don't . . ."

"Do you really want to know?"

"Well, it's not . . ."

"I'll tell you. I want to know why she bothered. I want to know why she took it upon herself to teach him how to be."

The rainstorm opened out in fat drops that splattered against the glossy leaves and filled the voices of tree frogs with enthusiasm.

"I want to know why she killed him."

Mr. Bates measured his remarks like a man buying land near an unstable frontier. He admitted they may not have understood what their children needed from them. She was a missionary's daughter; perhaps she was lonely? Perhaps she was left too much by herself, left caulking the walls of their compound with her young womanhood? What else could she do?

"Why him?"

"Maybe she loved him?"

Detective Sergeant Xlong plucked at the gummy chips of hors d'oeuvres still clinging to his elbow.

"What do you mean by that?"

Mr. Bates lowered his eyes before the policeman's gaze. He said he was sorry about his brother, and he was also sorry about his own son. But it was not his fault. He had done what he could. He had tried to raise Philip to be a successful member of society. He didn't know what had gone wrong. He had had to work hard; there had been too little time.

Detective Sergeant Xlong nodded. He understood work. The waiter appeared with a fresh plate of appetizers, but the policeman waved him away.

The rainstorm had passed the peak of its intensity. Mr. Bates sipped his Scotch. Had the thought occurred to him that he was confessing his pain at the failure of his son to live properly? The detective sergeant was sorry his little friend from Hong Kong wasn't there to appreciate his success. Mr. Bates hesitated, but the situation had been approached. Moule would approve; she said things ought to be brought out into the open. The policeman wondered if he shouldn't move more rapidly toward the coming confrontation with food.

The rain lifted; insects again began bellowing for love. Detective Sergeant Xlong ordered another round of drinks, pleased that he had regained his basic role as protective interrogator.

For Fing, the crisis had arrived when Cynthia decided his kris was a pagan idol. She insisted it had become a block between them, a tool of savagery binding him to his past. She explained that they didn't use such things in California, and Fing had traveled far enough down the road of uncertainty not to risk asking what they did use. He would have to get rid of it. Fing had balked. This was the hardest thing that could be required of a warrior, particularly a young one. The wavy-bladed knife represented his manhood.

135

Cynthia sulked, but she knew she had been called. She said she would have thought he'd found safety enough in the hands of the Lord.

Fing said he did, but upriver there were men who'd split him open as soon as look at him.

He wasn't going upriver again. He was going to stay with her and be her little brother-lover in Jesus. They were going to arrive at the Gates hand in hand and innocent as lambs.

Fing had argued that the knife was also useful for slaughtering game, cutting stakes, cleaning fingernails, a dozen other chores . . .

It had grown into an impasse; they parted without reaching an understanding.

The three brothers had returned upriver that afternoon. Fing's eyes were lit with a grim determination. She had told him he'd never be saved; he felt that had released him from her. Detective Sergeant Xlong and his younger brother could hardly contain their pleasure at his return.

After dinner, Fing sang a comic song. He curled his tongue and wiggled his ears. He said he couldn't wait for the dark. Everybody knew what that meant. He smeared pig fat on the blade of his kris and strutted the length of the porch, his eyes glittering. He's back! the younger boys shouted joyfully. Fing's back!

Fing had a hollow section of wet bamboo he slapped between his palms, *whomp whomp whomp,* splattering drops of moisture as he established a rhythm.

The unmarried women tittered and tried to force one another to climb down the notched log that led into the jungle. Fing paced to the end rail, turned, and started back down the long porch. The younger boys clutched themselves in anticipation. Fing reached the near rail and stopped. He had lost the slightest edge to his swagger, although probably only Detective Sergeant Xlong noticed. The other boys shouted encouragement as Fing passed, but the middle brother's stomach felt as if he had swallowed sand. Fing was only going through the motions. He was beating on his bamboo drum as if that might settle him back, but the sound was empty; he was lost, and he knew it.

He entered the night jungle eventually. By then others had recognized his reluctance, and the puzzled faces of the young women trudging up for breakfast the following morning provided final proof of his devastation.

That second day, Fing refused to eat. He squatted on the mud bank below their kampong and stared at the river. The younger boys kept a vigil on the longhouse porch. Bird flights, the grain of freshly split wood, the patterns of seeds spilled from their pods—every possible omen was examined for a way out. Nothing offered itself.

He sat all day under the sun. An aunt took him water and some gruel; he didn't notice. Fing! the younger boys shouted, crisp with dread. Fing! Come back!

He didn't move.

At last, with dusk settling over the river, he stood trembling to his toes, his face pressed toward the dying sky. He turned once toward the boys on the porch, his eyes blasted with pain and guilt at the betrayal, then spun with a single motion and threw his kris far out into the river.

"We watched that splash, Mr. Bates, surprised by how simply it was washed under the green skin of the river.

137

We had lost Fing; and although we were too young to realize it, from that moment, our way of life would begin to change.

"During the night, Fing followed the river to town. He never returned. The moisture was drained from his tissues; he became like a paper creature and rustled when he walked. We younger boys continued to go into town. Every time we saw him, he was drier, more brittle, and the previously friendly blades of our kampong fire would have consumed him in an instant."

George Bates excused himself and left the table. The policeman wondered if he had allowed his voice to fill unduly with remorse. Was the management of human emotion more than a technical problem? He might ask Moule; she could be trusted to have something to say.

◆((◆((◆((◆((◆((◆((◆((

They had spoken of Christian Funding as they took up his brother. Their voices were as calm and loving as the heavy wool felt glued to the bottom of their collection pot. Fing was to be given a chance to help. They draped him in skins. They changed his hair style to something never before seen. They painted on extra scar marks and puffed out his cheeks with mud. Each contributed in his own way, they told him.

They had taken a series of photographs, starting with him peering bug-eyed out of the brush and ending with him saved. Here he was without any hair, wielding the Lord's mop. And here he was happily hunched over a mound of the shoes of the servants of the Lord, polishing.

Detective Sergeant Xlong could have told George Bates that he had often heard of California, for it was there they published *Today's Crusader*, the missionary journal dedicated to such adventures as that undergone by his brother, and a convenient organ through which His servants could tap into the Lord's Cash Flow.

Cynthia had made the mistake of showing Fing the article. He had perhaps believed she wanted the photographs as keepsakes to place on the nightstand beside her bed. At that moment, he must have realized how badly he'd misunderstood.

Buried in a drawer of Detective Sergeant Xlong's police desk were the yellow sheets of print, swollen with years of rain. Beneath a picture of Cynthia teaching Fing how to fold clothes was the caption, "Crude Stone Age savage, bewildered by weakness and passion, in response to your gifts and prayers, finds relief at last in the life-restoring laundry room of the Lord."

Fing had hit Cynthia with a prayer bench. She collapsed at his feet. With a bellow of pain, he fled into the street. He struck in blind rage at anyone he met. He was soon on a classical amok, slashing through town, attacking everything in sight.

At that time, the colonial office had its militia barracks at the center of an open square. This was where Fing made his last stand, after bodily ejecting the surprised militiamen. The barracks was a solid building constructed of mud walls a meter thick. The roof was flat and surrounded by a low parapet with slits to shoot through. Fing barricaded all the doors and windows, then dragged rifles and ammunition up onto the roof.

The native militiamen tried an immediate counter-attack, rushing the barracks from three sides. The court-yard was too wide, however, and Fing managed to defend the building, driving them back with lucky shots that wounded four and killed a fifth outright.

At that, all attacks halted. The sight of their dead com-rade crumpled in the middle of the empty courtyard filled the militiamen with patience.

They set a siege. At night there were bonfires to make sure he couldn't escape under cover of darkness. He had no shade, no food, and, most important, no drinking water. There was never any doubt as to the outcome. Few thought he would be able to stand more than a couple of hours under the blazing tropical sun; but he hung on for three days, as much a prisoner of his grief as of the local militia.

Late in the morning of the fourth day, with the sun high above the jungle canopy, he jumped from the roof. He had a loaded rifle in each hand; perhaps he was hoping to shoot his way out of the trap. He broke both ankles on the hard dirt of the courtyard. The militiamen riddled his body with dozens of unnecessary rounds, frustrated at having been denied their beds.

Detective Sergeant Xlong added that in most cases the exaggerated nature of a violent response could be linked to the weather.

George Bates stared at him for a moment, then stood and crossed to the end of the veranda. He watched the last clouds break apart; the storm had completely passed. He glanced back at the policeman still sunk wearily in his chair, chin on his chest and cap tugged down over his eyes.

"The weather?" he said.

Detective Sergeant Xlong nodded without looking up. He knew a sense of guilt must be a terrible thing to one who couldn't accept it largely in climatological terms. Why was Mr. Bates's son so afraid? Why was his son so full of self-hatred? The troubled parent had nowhere to turn except inward. Detective Sergeant Xlong himself had always attempted to take comfort in the sun in the morning and the moon at night. "Because of the rain"—was the basic answer available here. The problem, then, became a matter of correctly couching each question. Something such as why the river rose and destroyed the crops was most satisfying. Indeed, it was possible to look forward to natural disasters as demonstrations of the reliable nature of the universe—without, of course, neglecting to bemoan the resultant famine.

There *were* standards, after all.

"My younger brother and I were required to remove the corpse," the policeman resumed. "We were told to hurry if we wanted to save him from scavengers. We kicked away the carrion birds with tears in our eyes. We wrapped him in bark cloth and wound him with vines. A single vulture hopped after us. I can remember how the tips of its wing feathers were frayed. I have always hated them, but never more than at that moment. On our way to the river, we had to pass the missionary compound. Cynthia was seated on the porch of the headmaster's house, her head dressed in a turban of white gauze.

"At the sight of her, I was filled with fear. I was afraid she might know what we were carrying. I was afraid she might not know. I was afraid I might have to speak to

141

her; for although her eyes were red from weeping, she still managed to watch us almost calmly.

"That, however, wasn't to be. The hatred of my little brother—a quality that fills him to this day—drove all before it. His small body shook with a rage he couldn't express. His end of the corpse slipped from his fingers as he started toward the house. Cynthia rose from her chair. Her face was pale but still unafraid. She called to her Chinese *amah* who was working in the room behind her.

"My brother mounted the stairs. He held one hand in front of him like a child lost in a nightmare. Cynthia was backed against the wall, but she said nothing. Standing before her, his fists knotted into two stones of grief, he could find no words that would balance the outrage he felt.

"He had nothing, no power. Finally he stripped off his school pants and threw them at her feet. He stood naked before her, his eyes burning with tears; but the gesture was too small, so he turned and fled into the jungle, ashamed of his impotence.

"I was left alone at the foot of the stairs. The vulture hopped forward awkwardly. Cynthia looked at me; her face was the color of paper. I understood then that I could still go to their school. I became filled with disgust at myself, for I knew what would happen. I picked up Fing and staggered, smashing through the brush, all the way to the river. I felt blinded; I knew intuitively how easily we were destroyed.

"You can understand that my younger brother gave up all interest in art. He never drew again. You can appreciate his emotion at his first rifle—an old bolt-action war surplus weapon so heavy he could barely lift it. You can perhaps picture him tugging and scratching at the mud, dragging the rifle and its boxes of ammunition wherever he went—even carrying it into his hammock with him as the only medicine he had for sleep. Not a happy child, Mr. Bates, and in some ways perhaps similar to your son."

Detective Sergeant Xlong had been ashamed to go back to their longhouse, for he had done nothing to avenge his brother's death. He left the body at the edge of the compound and fled back downriver. He was huddled miserably in an alley when the police discovered him. They took him in. Even though he was only a child, they recognized some quality in his grief that suggested he had become one of them.

He was shy at first, bashful as a new bride. The police waited behind their smiles. They were supportive. They gave him time to adjust. He believed that because he had been able to see the situation from various angles, he was frozen into inaction. He could see the sincerity of Cynthia's sorrow; he could understand her father's need to fund the school; he could appreciate the nature of the accident; he was reasonable, reasonable—it gripped him like the walls of a prison.

He knew he had been peeled. What he'd lost was hatred.

He wanted to go to the school. He argued to himself that what he needed was to confront his new perspective directly, to batter against it with his fists—but he felt too weak, too inept. And deep inside himself, he liked what he was gaining.

He had stayed with the police until his father sent for him. The police had shown him how to be. They taught

him how to produce methodical arrangements and mar-
veled at his quickness with the lessons. They provided him
with the tools he needed to escape the chaos which had so
nearly drowned him. He had told them of his ability to
line up and they understood. They put their hands on
him. They nodded and smiled, and gave him the children
of prisoners for practice. Even after he had returned to
his home, he still spent all his free hours in the rooms of
the police—learning from their ability to simplify, sharing
their bland food, smiling at their comedies, appreciating
the monotonic nature of their tunes.

"I continued my education, Mr. Bates. I perfected the
police philosophy and soon felt at home with an orderly
program of my own design."

It was time, the policeman thought. He smiled to recall
how even the children of prisoners had recognized his
right; and how he, on his part, had treated them kindly.

The last of the rain-damaged leaves dropped to the
pavement with wet smacks. Would Moule be cooling herself by her open window? Detective Sergeant Xlong stood
up, suddenly energetic, surprising George Bates with his
recuperative powers. It was time.

"What orderly program?"

Detective Sergeant Xlong unbuttoned his trousers and
spread open the fly to tuck in his shirt. It was odd how
there was never any detectable damage. But time, he
thought, time, and examined himself in the glass door
with obvious satisfaction. It was a shame Moule was not
here. Wouldn't she smile sweetly now and crack her
knuckles? Wouldn't her kimono lift away from her belly,

exposing the surface to evaporation? She was fond of her policeman.

"What orderly program?"

Cinching his belt closed with a self-conscious flourish, Detective Sergeant Xlong took a step toward the foreigner. Wouldn't Moule's hands be crabbing down the front of her kimono? Perhaps, yet the thought itself was the greater pleasure.

Wouldn't Moule brush her breast against him in passing? Wouldn't she be pleading with him to come to her soon? Of course she would. She needed her policeman. Yet Moule in the flesh could never match the sentences he built out of her. A pinch of skin was never as satisfying as the phrase it could be wrapped in. Both were elastic, yet meat had a pushy way of intruding at odd moments.

"What do you mean, 'program'?"

"That there is a right way for everything to be," the policeman said. "That there are ethics, fitted simply to our world like a kind of light switch: off or on. That that which doesn't follow its proper way is to be bent for its own good. That this is what we do. That this is our job. We clear things up." He turned, gesturing with his trigger finger toward the expanding patch of blue sky. "We put things in order. Cynthia's lesson has been perfected by simplification. The multiplicity of choices that confused my elder brother is for me as clear as on and off, as I said, as in and out, up and down, male and, and, and, whatever."

George Bates shook his head. "It may have been wrong," he began, "but she . . ."

"Wrong?"

"That your brother couldn't appreciate what was at stake in the clash between two cultures."

"Wrong?"

"Things can't be reduced to such a simple form!"

"Simple? In a country with a climate so oppressive that . . ."

"Detective Sergeant! I really can't see how the ethics involved could possibly . . ."

". . . the United Nations Geological Survey team refused to . . ."

". . . be determined by the weather!"

". . . finish its expedition?"

They stared at each other. The policeman felt the cords of his neck swell. He and other sensitive members of the police were cautious in employing simple concepts like "right" and "wrong" because the civilian population tended to attach unnecessary baggage to them.

Police principles taught them to divide problems into two categories: those which could be bent straight, and those which were too brittle and thus beyond bending. Detective Sergeant Xlong explained that in his opinion Sprague was very likely in the latter category while Mr. Bates's son was still in the former.

If George Bates was uncomfortable with this explanation, he did not show it. He calmly asked what the police did with those in the latter category, the ones beyond.

The policeman joined him at the rail. He draped a friendly arm around the foreigner's shoulders, his heavy face oozing sweat. He leaned on Mr. Bates, humming bits of Moule's favorite tune and wondering if the foreigner was able to appreciate the humor of their situation—for anyone spying on them from the street below would surely assume that they were friends.

"Bend them," the policeman said clearly. "Bend them anyway."

George Bates retained his composure. He swallowed and pulled back slightly. The policeman shifted his weight away from Mr. Bates and released his shoulder. He told himself it did not surprise him that there was still considerable distance to be covered. No one did well in this weather.

Detective Sergeant Xlong limped ponderously back to the table. The wooden floor of the veranda steamed, swelling in the moist heat. Mr. Bates still clung to the rail. As the policeman turned to signal toward the waiter, he detected the first faint strains of "Moon River." If it hadn't been for his sense of duty, he would have retired to a solitary corner and given himself over to the pleasure of memories of Moule. He smiled to think how affection was always at its best when one was alone to spread it open and enjoy it.

The wet walls of the hotel, too, had begun to expand. It was time to get on with the investigation. The policeman would agree with George Bates that a distinguishing feature of the human condition was the power to make choices, and that this was what led to perplexity—for he himself was continually torn between the drama of maintaining a steep angle on the bill of his cap and the ability to see. Nevertheless, he would argue, this free will business could dribble into troubling corners if there wasn't a man with a badge and a method in hand, willing to take responsibility for the actions of others.

147

You stand here, and you stand over there: how often had he used such phrases? Once you got everybody lined up, you had a good chance of being able to be alone. Organization—sometimes a simple census itself was enough. There's nothing like being counted to make a citizen sit up straight. One puts his name among the names of others. It's like he's owned; he knows where he belongs.

Some food, a friend, and the loaded side arm—wasn't there another term Moule added to his list? It slipped away like foam on the face of the river. He would have to ask her again.

"The police are now my family, it is true. Their history is my own. And the enemies of the police are now my enemies. Yes, Mr. Bates, does that suggest I admit my younger brother is now with the rebels? An excellent question."

The policeman recognized, of course, that Mr. Bates had not asked it. Sometimes it seemed as if he had to do everything himself. He turned to observe his reflection in the glass door again, but could make out nothing above his waist. He assumed Mr. Bates was still having difficulty with what must appear to be a setback. This, however, was not the case. They had communicated—imperfectly, perhaps, but firmly.

Pushing back his cap, Detective Sergeant Xlong picked up one of the jellied snake eggs which had collected beside his glass. It was time for a touch of police magic. He held up the slick black sphere and squeezed. The skin ruptured with a sudden slurp and the tiny fetus landed on the wet floor between them. The policeman wondered if Moule would find such a self-conscious display technically awkward. She tended toward spontaneity. Time was growing short, however, and Mr. Bates was still far from integrating himself.

"You wouldn't enjoy my brother; he hates foreigners. We of the police control the town and the nearby jungles; but farther out, uncertainty prevails."

He tossed the ruptured shell on the floor with a casual motion. George Bates had stiffened in response to the policeman's gesture.

"We've organized in order to protect ourselves. A spirit of community is a comforting thing, Mr. Bates. It's as simple as that."

Detective Sergeant Xlong pretended to be on the verge of departing. He turned toward the door, but instead of leaving, he crossed deliberately to the fetus puddled at Mr. Bates's feet.

The policeman sucked loudly on his teeth. He stooped forward, his arms hanging heavily before him like two clubs. "Do you like your son's friends?" he asked. Mr. Bates winced but said nothing. "Don't you have to choose?" The policeman placed his foot above the tiny fetus and began to crush it.

"Stop!" George Bates blurted out.

"It isn't alive."

"I don't care."

The policeman smiled. He didn't remove his foot. Would George Bates never guess that the little drama had been choreographed specifically to instruct him? Human vulnerability was placed within the concept of acting alone. The detective sergeant's head came forward from the lengthening stalk of his neck. "It's dead," he said slowly, grinding the fetus under the sole of his boot until not even a smear could be distinguished. "And you son isn't."

George Bates raised one hand to his throat. He stared into the policeman's face. Detective Sergeant Xlong almost held his breath. Would the foreigner be wondering if he shouldn't find some way to congratulate him on the handling of a difficult piece of police artifice? It seemed unlikely.

. . . crossing you in time, someda-a-ay . . .

The policeman sucked the interstices between his teeth dry as George Bates struggled with doubt.

The side wall of the veranda had continued to expand, bloating out thick and green with the soft fuzz of new mold. Eventually this outer wall would crumble away, and the hotel would collapse in on top of it.

Detective Sergeant Xlong still had not moved. Hunched as he was, his weight pulled his heavy shoulders forward. But instead of giving the appearance of a beast about to spring, he looked more like one attempting to suppress an attack of nausea.

"Sprague?" George Bates sighed.

"Right!" the policeman said, making no effort to hide his pleasure. "Sprague is the key. But first, lunch!" he shouted toward the waiter sagging in the doorway. "And more Scotch for Mr. Bates and more whiskey for me! And put it all, all on the bill of the police!"

Clearly, an occasional pleasure flowered during the

course of the police day. Was it the policeman's joy at the ostensible compliance that deadened his receptors? Why else would he have missed so many clues? What else could have so coated his intuition that he had no inkling of his younger brother—his anger at last heating toward the point of no return—slogging through the mud to the refrain that it was time, time, time.

Was he simply too innocent? He would have to ask himself why he had had no sense of the figures advancing on the bathing beach upriver—the group of three following the path; and the fourth, the smaller one, the darker one, the one like him delivered down the chute of a mother's groans into the green arms of stagnant water; the one who under his loving eye had sharpened his first stick, strangled his first weasel; the one who had at last been driven to sliding through the jungle, trying to silence the heartbeat of doubts that ticked inside him, counting that it was time, now, time, time to act.

What could the policeman have known, other than that the people would build a new hotel on the failure of the old one? And that its walls, too, filled with moisture, would swell and bulge and decay?

The waiter appeared in the doorway with a covered platter. George Bates watched the policeman warily but with no overt hostility.

Detective Sergeant Xlong knew his niece had returned upriver. On a better day, he might have been able to sense her clothing dropped at the water's edge, and Philip and her father drawing more deeply into the vortex of their atrocious dance; he might have been able to intuit the murderer pressing himself in anticipation of vengeance or, perhaps, simply of being at last on the rim of his own death.

The policeman lifted the lid. "What's that?" he wondered aloud, no doubt too self-conscious at the promise of their coming shared meal. "Is that some sort of fish?" The waiter scurried back to the kitchen to ask.

What could they have known? Only that people would stand in the street and watch as a new hotel fell slowly into the hole of an old one. Nothing lasted in the Republic. Each isolated mud brick would slip free from its mortar to drop leisurely, soundlessly, end over end—bricks first squeezed from jungle clay by the rogue geologist as a gesture toward civic improvement; bricks held up as an example of Western utilitarianism to those who had had an identical lesson conveyed initially with dynamite; bricks, the foundation row of which were laid in a ceremony by the geologist himself, laid with a speech on how even the jungle could be squared up and made to do work; bricks, gifts, rewards for creeping back despite the explosions; bricks that for the people of the Archipelago had meaning then, and would continue to have meaning as they dropped silently, softly, slowly, one after the other, end over end over end, to land without sound back in the mud hole, back home.

No, Detective Sergeant Xlong heard no pistol shots. His attention was drawn to the coming need to properly manipulate a dining fork. The spaced reports were swallowed up by the soft heaviness of the jungle air, by his sudden indifference to the weather—the weather, the root

term for which in his language was the same as the word
for the skin.

❖❐❖❐❖❐❖❐❖❐❖❐❖❐

Hours passed, but still the question lingered: Moule?
Moule now?

No, he insisted to himself, clinging to his solitude,
struggling against the forces that lifted his shoulders up
against their wet khaki sacks and stiffened his neck. It
was time to be alone.

He had not disgraced himself at lunch. Nevertheless,
throughout the awkward course of the meal his muscles
had continued to fill with the realization that something
had happened—something beyond his immediate frame,
but something his, his business.

He had returned immediately after dessert, growing
agitated at the prospect of being within hours of results.
He had kicked his junior officers out of their hammocks,
produced the keys to the armory with a hurried flourish;
and, sure that he had everyone's attention, told them they
were about to be issued real bullets.

The electricity of the moment flowed through each man
in the squad room. Breaking the tapes off an ammunition
case, Detective Sergeant Xlong felt like the good father,
the provider. Hungers he had nurtured in his men were
now to be fed. This was one of the great rewards for the
senior officers of the police. There would be accidental
shootings, no doubt—flesh wounds, blasted toes, maybe
even an inadvertent fatality or two; but it was time to

screw the moment to its hole, time to throw his men into the struggle. He had told himself he had no choice, and smiled, and felt fine.

Now, alone in his empty office, he surveyed the neutral walls. Not even Moule had been able to say what color they were. "A sort of greenish gray beige," she'd decided with obvious distaste. She didn't understand that blandness was wanted for contrast with the outside world, for the distance an institution could establish between the detainee and his previous condition. It helped, the policeman had argued, to alter—in the first few moments of uncertainty—the fellow's attitude toward his sense of personal worth. This could go a long way in the extraction of information. A lot of trouble could be saved for everyone involved. One ought to do what one could to ease the situation.

Moule had not been impressed by his generosity. He wondered sometimes why they had their little misunderstandings.

Detective Sergeant Xlong had painted a rainbow of lines down the central corridor, each different color leading to a separate interrogation room. He explained that this provided a useful sense of false distinction, for although each room was identical to the others, the lines suggested a systematization and thus allowed rumors to circulate. Fears clustered around the nature of the unstringing to be encountered, say, at the end of the orange line—his favorite, selected, of course, arbitrarily. Myth made mystery, as useful for ordering as the human fist—more, as a matter of fact, since the secondary effects had a wider extension. Another line was the most successful, however. A deep and frequently repainted dull gray, it led to the door of an unused storage closet. Although thus never employed, it was the most respected—due, no doubt, to the constant extra maintenance.

"Distinction," he had explained, "combined with the thumb of the capricious."

Moule had shaken her head at that. She said sometimes she just felt that maybe she'd been in this damn town too long.

"The weather," the detective sergeant had told her.

She hadn't answered.

Now the policeman was alone. Was this a good world? he wondered. Was this the proper world for a man? He stroked the wet leather of his holster. It was a dirty job, he smiled. Such a dirty job, but somebody had to do it. The hours were long; the pay was bad. This was what he knew one should think, although the idea of being off duty held no meaning for him, and he'd rarely found much use for his salary. What did one buy? He'd looked in the markets; he'd visited all the shops. Everything seemed fine, but why would one want to go to the trouble of carrying a lot of extra objects about? He'd studied a fancy shirt once and tried to imagine owning it. Nothing came. It was just there, hanging limply from his hands, lifeless, static, blank. He had no idea how much he was paid since he threw away most of his money when it got to be too much of a lump in his pocket.

And danger bloomed in every unlit alley, this was another thing that could be said by the police. His enemies were everywhere—or rather, he would always feel obliged to correct, everywhere beyond the bite of his perimeter— for he had been busy; he had been careful to apply some of the essentials. And he had had his little successes.

Still, it was comforting that there were negative things one could say about life in the police. Outsiders could sense the orderly nature of the universe suspended from the hinges of the fact that members of the force had complaints. Detective Sergeant Xlong knew popular movies from Los Angeles frequently celebrated the lives and trials of policemen. He would have given his best pistol to hear Mr. Bates recount one of these, but he could hardly bring himself to ask. He was too shy, entirely too shy.

His eyes were heavy; he dozed. He tried to pretend he was sitting in a darkened theater, watching his life on the screen; but he had no feeling for what it meant to be in a movie, so he had to settle for the blurred patterns inside his eyelids.

He was sleepy. Where was little Moule? Back in her room with a wet towel? He was dozing.

Crack! He'd been dreaming. He heard scraping as he swam up toward the light. *Crack*—he was fully awake. The sound was beyond his window.

He kept his back to the wall, sidling toward the open space. His gun was in his hand. Was it loaded? He couldn't remember. There was a rubbing against the outside wall. Someone was below his open window.

He glanced out. Nothing, no shots. He could still hear a scuffling on the other side of the wall. He cocked back the hammer and threw himself into the open window.

Nothing. No one was there. The courtyard was empty.

The sound came from directly below him. He leaned out the window. A vulture with a broken wing floundered helplessly against the wall of the police barracks. It twisted its head up toward him and blinked a single ruby eye. Its beak cracked open, a single torn flap of skin hanging off from one side. It hissed slowly, purposefully, blood rattling out the open side of its damaged beak, the action one of pure reptilian hatred.

Detective Sergeant Xlong jerked back from the window, shocked by the nearness of the bird. He yanked open the door and lunged into the center of the courtyard. The vulture was trapped against the wall. It tried to get away, hopping sideways and tripping over its smashed wing. He pursued it carefully, blocking any lane of escape. It stopped, backed into a corner, standing on its own wing. As he came closer it hissed again, the insides of its white mouth puffy as dirty cotton, the blood bubbling out of the wound in its throat.

The policeman held the pistol in both hands and again cocked back the hammer. He aimed at the back of the bird's open mouth and squeezed the trigger. The hammer snapped against the strike plate. He cocked the hammer and tried again. Nothing; the cylinder was empty.

The bird glared at him. It hated him, and he hated it in the same way. He backed off. He had bullets in a leather case on his belt. He flicked the release on his pistol and the cylinder dropped open. He stared at the bird and his rage slowly passed. It was maimed; it would be dead by nightfall. Was that a thing to take comfort in? He felt a sudden wave of self-consciousness and quickly glanced behind him. Nobody was there. Why did he care? He closed the cylinder and holstered his still unloaded pistol. He didn't know why he cared. He had the feeling someone was watching him. What would Moule think? He backed farther off, then turned toward the door. But what if someone could see him? Why *did* he care? Was he a policeman or wasn't he? It was his job to protect the public against dangerous creatures.

He looked back at the bird. It was still standing stupidly on its wing. Its ugliness nauseated him. A sudden, deeply seated fear rolled up through his back; and he saw his entire world squeezed down into that crippled, mindless bit of hatred. He snatched his pistol out with one hand and fumbled at the case of bullets with the other, ripping at the flap so violently that the bullets splashed out onto the dirt of the courtyard.

He fell to his knees. He was having trouble seeing. He patted at the dirt until he found a single bullet and slipped it into the cylinder.

His father was dead, he told himself. His grandfather was dead; his great-grandfather was dead. He lay on his stomach to steady his shaking hands. His mother had walked into the river one day and been swept away. He rotated the cylinder so that the shell would come directly under the cocked hammer. His grandfather had died of a knife wound in the neck, and his father had died of bad food—the few teeth he had snapping off as he squirmed against the pain.

The policeman didn't think he could still see the bird. But he could hear its struggling. That would be enough.

The wave of who he was roared up his back again, flattening him and filling the skin over his shoulders with the endless feet of his ancestors. He sensed their absence flowing through him. There had been more deaths in the world than grains of sand. Wouldn't it be time for one more? The voices of the dead dragged along his neck like wet strings of yellow grass. It was time, time.

He knew the pistol was cocked in his hand, yet he had never felt so porous. Which direction was the river? Where was the police barracks in which he had stroked his loneliness into a ready weapon? If he knew where he was, couldn't he pull the trigger?

He was still hoping for an answer when the vulture came for him. It had knocked itself over and rolled onto its back, one claw grasping at the empty afternoon sky. Then, as he waited, it struggled to its feet with its wing untangled and started moving toward him, its beak cracked open, the dead wing dragging at an impossible angle.

The policeman felt himself being wrung by lack. Hatred had been drained from the eyes of the vulture, as if it, too, had momentarily experienced itself as little more than a conduit. It staggered awkwardly. As it passed, the dead wing brushed against the detective sergeant's shoulder; he was marked by it, like food trapped within the shell of its label.

He could hear the scuffing crunch as the bird departed. Was it heading toward the river? He settled into the soundlessness of his own family, also beginning to depart, also not looking back.

He knew he was always going to be alone.

❖❈❖❈❖❈❖❈❖❈❖❈❖❈

"Napping in your clothes? But don't you know your sweat will dry into the fabric and chill you?"

"What? What time . . . ?"

"And we, your friends in the police, have practically solved this complicated case. No, don't thank us yet. Although a few loose ends remain, the crime, at least, has shown itself at last, opened its skirt flaps like a shy child.

"A nasty business, Mr. Bates, nasty even for here; love and intrigue, murder and deceit, hopeless flight, pointless struggle—the essential contours of the jungle tragedy are exposed for our fingers; irreversible now, I might add; while you, our witness and companion, a principal in this matter, have been sleeping."

The policeman tossed his cap on the bed with an expansive gesture. Some sections, he would have to admit, were less available than others. Nevertheless, without worrying about the details overmuch, they could talk in terms of making arrests, picking up evidence, extracting voluntary confessions, and recording how the pieces fell together.

"I've, I've been asleep."

Detective Sergeant Xlong sank to the foot of the bed. He restrained himself; he knew stretching out with his head on the pillow would be inappropriate. He rapped a familiar fist against George Bates's ankle.

"He's in love—that's what I'd been missing. Oh, indeed, a technical matter, you'll be telling yourself, but one that's as slippery as a fish, Mr. Bates, as tough to stopper as a live eel—romantic love, I mean, you understand: our so-called 'Sensuality comma Human'—always sticky, as I've mentioned before, and a frequent source of confusion to members of the police."

"What the . . . what time is it?"

"Night."

"What're you doing here?"

"In love, Mr. Bates, as I said, and . . ."

"That door was locked!"

Granted, of course, but the policeman believed a forced lock should never come between friends. He would have liked to explain how they'd shared too much to quibble over details now that the necessary corner of crime had been rounded; but he understood George Bates could not close around success as easily as he could—trapped, as the foreigner was, in an inflexible system; so he restrained himself, scraped a crescent of trash from beneath the crease of his thumbnail, and mentioned that Berthe's father had been gunned down before her very eyes, adding that it might be to Mr. Bates's advantage to inquire as to the identity of the person suspected by the daughter of the victim to be guilty.

George Bates pushed past the policeman and went into the bathroom to wash his face. The lump on his forehead had become the same greenish purple as the one under his eye.

When he returned to the room, Detective Sergeant

Xlong was standing just inside the doorway, his niece clutched before him in both hands. The young woman seemed totally exhausted. Her arms hung limply at her sides as she sagged against her uncle. Her eyes hardly focused and her face was swollen with tears. She looked at nothing.

"Berthe Xlong, Mr. Bates, my niece. We call her Xlong to help her remember she belongs to her mother."

"We've met," George Bates said, evidently confused by the presence of the grieving woman.

"I know. Did you think I didn't know? Did you think I hadn't found out about that letter? I've been waiting for you to show it to me. You can still do so voluntarily."

George Bates ignored the policeman. He cleared his belongings off the only chair in the room. Detective Sergeant Xlong released Berthe and she sank into the chair, her hand shading her eyes as her head settled against the back.

"Can I get you something?"

"She probably doesn't want anything. But I might have something. Why don't you ask me?"

"She's all wet and muddy, and her clothes are torn. What happened?"

"Of course we could call room service. You could order something. Or I could order something."

"What the hell do you want from me?"

"Mr. Bates! Don't you understand? The case is cracked!"

"You're impossible!"

"Oh, she'll tell you that your son is the victim of a hoax, you can count on that. No accusations from her. She'll insist she doesn't know the name of the true criminal. We can be sure she has every intention of protecting Philip; but in her efforts to do so, she may precipitate the very tragedy she's trying to avert.

"You'd lie for him, wouldn't you, Xlong? Even though in your heart you believe he's guilty."

"He's innocent!" the young woman blurted out, her eyes momentarily flaring with anger.

"You see, Mr. Bates? She doesn't trust us. We have no choice but to work together.

"You might trust Mr. Bates; am I right, Xlong? You might think he could do something to help you.

"Understand, Mr. Bates, that the key to my niece is her mother. The geologist and his wife did not get along. Poor Xlong was always caught in the middle, for she loved them both.

"If not Philip, then it must be someone else; do you agree, Xlong? And even if him, who put him up to it? And if not him, who then?

"This, Mr. Bates, is the basic form of interrogation. One asks questions from various angles.

"You might be protecting your mother; am I right, Xlong? You might think she's the one who had your father killed."

"Detective Sergeant!"

"You don't know her, Mr. Bates. She's clever. In that respect she takes after her mother. The women in my family have always been devious, while the men . . ."

"Leave her alone!"

"Mr. Bates . . ."

"I mean it!"

There was a shouting in the hall, followed by a crash, as if part of the wall had fallen in. Detective Sergeant Xlong seized his niece by one wrist and dragged her out of the room. After a brief silence, the excited voices began again. Before George Bates could investigate, the policeman returned without his niece.

"Only a rat." He smiled, blocking the doorway. "A large one the employees claim has been stealing their food. Some of them are diverting it while others go for weapons."

"Where's your niece?"

"We can examine her again after she has rested."

"But where is she?"

"That stupid rat fell through a hole in the ceiling!" The policeman chuckled. "Everyone was very surprised."

"I don't give a damn about any rat!"

Detective Sergeant Xlong squared his cap. He was patient. He would be willing to explain again that Mr. Bates was mistaking the way things occurred here. With the arrival of the crime, he himself had suddenly felt cleansed. Process would prevail. That was enough. Things would blend together and become perfect, become whole, mild, liquid—if not his. He had been tempted by a yearning to possess. An act of friendship, an act of murder—they were in their own way as deadly to the soul as a lust for merchandise. He realized how vulnerable he had been. But no more. He was wide awake.

He explained that in his opinion Philip might have met Xlong's mother, his sister—her name, too, being Xlong. The sharing of a name provided a measure of group identity—an intimacy of the finest kind, helping one, as it did, to avoid the danger of seeing oneself as unique.

"Why don't you leave me alone? Just get the hell out of here and leave me alone!"

The policeman nodded. He adjusted his cap again. At that moment a squad of hotel employees charged past the open door. The leaders were armed with axes and chopping knives, but most only carried chunks of brick.

Detective Sergeant Xlong had certain knowledge as to why people became unhappy. It was their belief that the things of this world had value. Puzzled though he often was by odd events—usually in the company of his little friend from Hong Kong—nevertheless, he insisted, the human was perfectible. Bliss was just around the corner. All you had to do was surrender your stubborn ego and do what you were told.

"Let's talk about it later, do you mind?"

The men who had remained at the far end of the hall sent up a shout of relief. No doubt they were overjoyed by the sight of their returning comrades.

"We become dissatisfied with our lives because we cling to this world."

George Bates jerked open the door.

"Do you suppose it could be argued that your son was merely seeking a spiritual path? And that his quest just became tangled up in commerce and crime along the way?"

Mr. Bates stood beside the open door. He said nothing.

"A possible defense, Mr. Bates. You can appreciate that I'm trying to place this matter in a wider frame."

A howl of disappointment rose at the far end of the

165

hall. The rat had evidently fought its way to freedom.

"That's a pity," the policeman said, departing. "No food will be safe here."

George Bates slammed the door behind him.

❖❖❖❖❖❖❖❖❖❖❖

"First: everyone is an accessory."

A junior officer raised his face and blinked for a moment, then went back to sleep. Harsh light from the interrogation lamp overhead deadened the air. Detective Sergeant Xlong picked up a pencil to tap. He'd seldom felt better. Weapons on the wall, a hammock stowed in its locker, junior officers arranged on wooden chairs around his desk —what more could a man want? He felt fine. Sets of explanations foamed up within him, sure signs of good health.

"Second . . ." He paused, but no one awoke. Sprague scraped above them. The detective sergeant could hear the man's fingernails tearing steadily at the wood around the hasp of his door. He knew he could count on Sprague to attempt an escape. The man was wonderfully predictable.

Detective Sergeant Xlong drew his pistol and began disassembling it. There would be shooting tomorrow, he was sure of that. Philip had hated the upriver jungles at first, but the smeltery had become more like home than the country he had abandoned. He had written that it was as if the world upriver shimmered. The focus became blurred with humidity; things merged together. Borders lost their blades. Questions meant less, and washed against themselves until they overlapped. The boy might fight.

Philip had written that life in L.A. was like a photograph so finely developed that each line carved out its separate shape as menacingly as a razor. Here, however, the camera was underwater, and Philip found that comforting. Wasn't this the key to the crime? Couldn't his acclimatization have been so thoroughly completed that fatal events flowed out of it?

Perhaps, the policeman concluded. But murder wasn't really very ambiguous.

He stood and crossed to the window. He would visit little Moule later. Someone had left a bayonet on the windowsill. This was a good life. Everything was suggestive.

Philip had written of afternoons spent wandering in the ruins. He didn't mention whether Berthe was included in those jaunts among sunlit piles of stone or not. He had described heaps of severed tendrils drying in courtyards like green fingers waiting to be burned, but not a word of a human companion.

The policeman had always thought of his niece as a child, but that would have to be revised now. She had grown into a woman. If she had accompanied Philip on his sightseeing, she would have discovered the history of her clan carved the length of the temple walls. Would she understand how once again the violator had arrived from beyond the sea? Wouldn't she have found her father made anew in Philip, and understood that Mr. Bates's son could be a chance to repair the damage inflicted by the former?

Perhaps. But she was still young. It might not have

167

occurred to her to make a gift out of Philip. She might have simply followed him into the ruins and allowed herself to be undressed. Did Philip perch her on a slab of stone to see her nakedness in the sunlight the way the geologist had made love to her mother?

The policeman bent abruptly and fitted the bayonet into his boot top. He had stumbled upon his sister and her lover in the ruins. He had been amazed at the way the geologist pawed and rubbed her, at the way he insisted upon looking at everything, the way he ate things with his eyes, the way he studied her body like a man looking for something he'd lost without ever having known he could have it.

Detective Sergeant Xlong tried walking with the bayonet in his boot, but it was too awkward. It would fall out immediately under battle conditions.

He had thought that he understood coupling, but he had come away from that daylight scene in the ruins so shaken that he believed he could never speak to his sister again. The foreigner lived through his eyes. His eyes had sucked at her; and even when he stroked her body, it was in order to see, to watch her change under the pressure of his fingertips.

The policeman returned to his chair. He felt suddenly tired. Should he wake one of his men? No, they needed their rest.

What did Philip find in the ruins? It must have been Berthe Xlong. It was the same again, the same violation. Yet the boy wrote about what he saw. He had described the amputated vines and concluded that he could accept a determination to preserve the ruins without any longer believing in it. But what did that mean? There was, Philip wrote, something sedative to be found in the historical works of man, some perfect form of peacefulness that was one of the characteristic signatures of a destroyed civilization—the point, as it were, of the ruins.

The policeman yawned. Fine, but where was his niece in all that perfect peace? He didn't know. He felt drowsy. He rubbed his eyes. Action. Tomorrow someone was going to resist arrest. The question of locating Mr. Bates's lost son remained, it was true. Yet he had to admit to himself that his heart was no longer much in the search. Perhaps he was just tired. Tomorrow he would feel more lively. Besides, the boy was involved in the crime—in which role hardly mattered. The dead would have to be buried. Reports would have to be filed, a trial kicked up, punishments attached—yet he realized that what had most deeply moved him was the sudden blooming of his niece. Would he then have to live through his sister's corruption a second time? He didn't know. But Berthe struck him as the last whole member of his family; and if it was for her that he would have to fight, he might do so with more than his usual enthusiasm.

He nodded. He shook his head to clear it, but he was tired. He felt forlorn. Where were the tongues of the dead that had flowed in his shoulders like river grass? Gone. He knew much would be asked of him. He felt alone, abandoned. Apparently even the dead died.

There was a crash above him; bits of wet plaster dropped from the ceiling. Sprague had broken out of his detainment cell. The policeman could hear the *clump-thump clump-thump* as he dragged himself toward the back stairs. Should he send a junior officer to kick awake his men? He felt too tired. His neck was stiff. Could he slog through the formality of yet another pursuit? Should he drag Sprague through another capture? The man was tough. He could stand it. But perhaps it was time to let Sprague settle to his own level.

Yes, Sprague would be considered pardoned. Charges would be dropped. There would be plenty of other wrongs. Detective Sergeant Xlong knew he would be occupied.

◆《◆《◆《◆《◆《◆《◆《

"Bobo?"

"What?"

"Are you going to sleep here tonight?"

"You know I don't sleep."

"Are you going to stay until the sun comes up?"

"No."

"Oh. Bobo?"

"What?"

"You make mistakes."

"Mistakes?"

"Do you think you're always right?"

"It's part of the duty of the members of the .

"Sometimes people think you're too pushy."

"Pushy?"

"Is that son so bad?"

"Probably not. Not as bad as the father."

"I don't think he's so bad."

"You like everybody."

"I like you."

"Oh."

"Do you think I'm nice?"

"You're nice."

"Do you want to put your hand on me?"

"Where?"

"Anywhere. On my breast?"

"Maybe not there."

"On my stomach?"

"For how long?"

"A few minutes? You might like it."

"Okay. Maybe later."

"Oh. But that means you're going to stay here awhile?"

"No."

"Oh. Bobo?"

"What?"

"Is that son really guilty?"

❖❖❖❖❖❖❖❖❖❖❖

"I can do anything I want! Anything! Do you hear? You can't stop me!"

Detective Sergeant Xlong stood uncovered in the rain. His cap was stuffed into the crotch of his police pants. The night storm lashed against his battered face, sheets of rain bouncing off, splashing over his soaked uniform. Waves of runoff rushed down the street, covering to the tops of his feet. The world was deserted. No one else was awake except George Bates standing in his window with his hair mussed and his jacket thrown over his shaking shoulders.

"Do you hear me?" the foreigner shouted again. "Anything!"

The policeman did not turn toward the window. Sunrise was less than two hours away. The memory of Moule flooded him with emotion. He lifted his arms and assumed the position of defense. He crouched slightly, shifting his weight onto the balls of his feet. He released a quick left jab; rain splattered off his fist. He circled to his left, threw another left, and another, then feinted slightly toward the right and came back with a wicked right uppercut. Rain blew in every direction. He threw combinations, left right left; he followed pairs of left jabs with right crosses. He leaned back, on the ropes, faking injury. He was reeling. The rain blew down. He circled to the wrong side and was suddenly boxing southpaw, jabbing out leading with his right fist, right jab right jab, his chin tucked up to his left shoulder, his left arm cocked, waiting for a clear shot, waiting for the moment, waiting for a chance to shoot in a left hook.

"I don't give a damn!" George Bates screamed from his window. "We're innocent! Damn it! Innocent! Innocent!"

four ᴵᶜᐧᴵᶜᐧᴵᶜᐧᴵᶜᐧᴵᶜᐧᴵᶜᐧᴵᶜᐧᴵᶜᐧᴵᶜᐧᴵᶜᐧᴵᶜᐧᴵᶜᐧᴵᶜᐧ

THE VALUE OF
A FRIEND IN THE POLICE

No, this was no killer. Intuition guided the policeman in such matters. The boy might approach the moment, slick with fear; but he lacked the necessary distance to pull the trigger. One needed an absence of imagination to kill. Philip dribbled into everyone he met. It would never do to see in oneself the shape of the other. The boy was as liquid as any foreigner Detective Sergeant Xlong had encountered.

The policeman cracked his knuckles and yawned. Was the investigation becoming a shade too predictable? Perhaps.

He studied the young man's face for traces of the rogue geologist. The compulsive hunger was absent, although lack of sleep may have been the cause of that.

Philip shook his head to the policeman's question. "Dead," he muttered, "dead."

Detective Sergeant Xlong eased back in his chair. He

could still recall the glow of the geologist's weapons on the day he arrived for his wedding. To a boy at the end of his schooling, the advent of that first foreigner had been overwhelming. The man had seemed filled with sunlight. His appearance must have been the determining factor in the middle brother's decision to dedicate himself to the National Police.

"He was repulsive!" Philip declared, showing animation for the first time. "He deserved it!"

"Philip!"

"Well, Mr. Bates, here we have . . ."

"He's just upset!"

Just upset? Just? The policeman nodded without further comment. This was not what he'd hoped for from the father. Mr. Bates wanted nothing to do with him. He even failed to comment on the successful stakeout which had rescued his son.

Nevertheless, the policeman continued to himself, that rogue geologist would be hard to replace. The boy sagging here shackled to a table hardly seemed a fit candidate. There was no grandeur in him. He wouldn't be the one to stand on the riverbank before setting out on a journey and lift his head and squeeze his eyes shut, silencing every member of the kampong, and raise his hands gradually over the face of the river in benediction. And if he did, would the flow appear finer at his demand? The color deeper? The foam more wonderful to the eye? It seemed unlikely.

They had learned from the geologist that the world could be made to obey. At first they had fought against the geological survey team he headed. They were no match for the automatic weapons of the invaders. The detective sergeant's father, in an excess of cunning, had sued for peace by offering his daughter as a gift to the team commander. They anticipated a polite refusal followed by withdrawal. They got neither.

For Plo-xlong, the wedding had been a second betrayal. He had never forgiven the death of Fing. Because he was only a child, he had not been allowed to take part in the attacks on the invaders. He refused to join the other children in their games and nursed his hatred alone.

On the day of the wedding, the geologist had ascended the river in glory. He stood in the bow of the lead canoe; no one had ever done that. He was tall and blond, and he dressed in uniforms covered with flapped pockets. He was white and gold, a rajah cradling an automatic rifle. Mr. Bates and his son could never appreciate how fulfilled the policeman had been by the sight of him. The geologist radiated power. Everything he touched appeared altered. He understood how the world worked, although Detective Sergeant Xlong was the only one in the kampong who could realize it. For the others, it was enough that the war was over and the golden rajah from beyond the sea had agreed to marry the headman's daughter. They glimpsed nothing of the disasters such a union could bring.

Although he was only a boy, the arrival had been crucial for the detective sergeant. He read it as a sign meant for him. He knew he had been singled out. He accepted that he had no choice, and waited for his message.

The policeman tried to make a friendly remark to George Bates. There was no answer. Mr. Bates obviously intended to ignore him as openly as possible. He would insist on nothing less than a private interview with his son. No doubt he wanted to help him establish a uniform presentation of the series of events that curved into the centrifugal moment of murder. In this he perhaps hoped they would become united—the concerned father guiding the distraught but grateful son. It could happen.

The policeman yawned again. Why was he suddenly so sleepy?

Poor Plo-xlong. That day of the wedding should have been his victory. He had hidden a bow and arrow in the shadows beneath the longhouse. All morning he had stalked the riverbank, clutching himself in anticipation. He was an excellent bowman; the arrowhead was poisoned. A scratch would be fatal. It must have seemed impossible that his revenge would be denied. He was so sure of fulfillment that he spoke to his brother for the first time since the death of Fing. Poor Plo-xlong; he had believed his demons were about to be brought to their knees.

The policeman observed George Bates picking at the mud caked on his shoes. How he must have raced through the wet gloom of the morning forest, pedaling furiously on his rented bicycle, hoping to overtake the detective sergeant and his squad. There had never been any question that Mr. Bates would arrive too late. He had no aptitude for crime—no lingering scent of black powder to suspend him above the lethargy of normal life; no shell casing discovered in the guilty pool of a footprint to drive him; nothing but the duty of the father—sprung from sleep by the urgent voice of Berthe Xlong telling him his son had been trapped.

The policeman sighed to think of Mr. Bates's surprise. Was there a training lesson here? The old man must have braced himself on damp elbows, his sheets wedged in sour cakes between his skinny thighs while the frightened young woman confessed her role in the homicide, poured out parts of the event the father would never have guessed at, and redrew the fatal triangle that had formed around her as she undressed on the riverbank.

Was it a scene police instructors would enjoy—dead insects scattered across the floor, the young woman amazed as the foreigner snatched up his pants and rushed off toward the bicycle rental shop? Mr. Bates would have refused to believe the policeman's niece when she told him he could accomplish nothing on his own. Only when he had rounded the bend in the trail and spotted his son sitting at a poorly constructed table and preparing to share a bit of brunch, perhaps, or a morning cocktail, perhaps, only then would he have realized that Berthe Xlong's warning might have been less spontaneous than he had assumed—and in that, too, he would be overreacting, condemning Berthe to the role of conspirator.

From the edge of the clearing, Mr. Bates could have recognized that the little jungle café was formed by two wings salvaged from a jet aircraft—an excellent roof, particularly in rain, provided one avoided the spaced leakage of bullet holes. The legend NO STEP was stenciled in several places—a bright yellow against the silver alloy wings, understandable, the policeman never failed to observe, as a kind of coded message meant for him alone: undeciphered, as of yet, but producing a measure of comfort nevertheless.

177

Mr. Bates had shown himself and approached the table cautiously. Although Detective Sergeant Xlong had been careful to allow them time in which to extend their initial greetings, both father and son had sunk into an awkward silence, embarrassed by each other's presence.

The policeman knew he could afford to be patient. There was every reason to suppose he would have his moment of satisfaction. His brother had gone too far. Although George Bates no doubt would have little interest in the refinements available, the policeman smiled to think of the concern the trigger man must be feeling for the nature of the tableau. There would be difficulties in explaining the political purity of the shooting of the father of a young woman exposed knee-deep and naked in a river. Poor Plo-xlong. He'd never get it back. The balance would continue to favor the police.

Shouldn't this have been sufficient? No doubt, yet the detective sergeant yearned to explain the dilemma to Mr. Bates. The smooth wet back and shining haunches of young Xlong—could Mr. Bates fail to appreciate what a poor piece of propaganda that would make? The innocent daughter soaping her belly while the assassin worked the cocking action on his pistol. Hardly the stuff dreams are made of. For the perpetrator, a tainted victory would seem no victory at all. The policeman smiled. It might merely appear to be nothing more than a bit of common voyeurism spurted out of control. It depended on how the elements were linked; and in the art of arranging, he knew he had no peer.

Detective Sergeant Xlong wiped his palms on his pants. Still, something wasn't quite right. This wasn't what he had expected. Philip looked, predictably enough, as if he were about to vomit. His face was pale and splotched from days of bad water. His muddy clothing clung to his back. Was he infested with insects? Probably. Had fungi established themselves in unattended quarters of his body? No doubt. Here parasites were enthusiastic, scrapping for any inch of flesh.

So the policeman had not been surprised by the degree of devastation, yet Philip's defiance had left him off balance. He had thought he might be able to drive the investigation to its conclusion right here at this little café. That now seemed much less likely.

The policeman was again tempted to approach the son through the father. Why couldn't Mr. Bates share their good fortune at the ramifications branching out from the murder? There was a meeting ground available if the elder foreigner would only agree to choose it. They could stand together as two men, two citizens, and speculate on the slackening consciousness of the dying geologist—his face partially submerged, the light peeling away in broken frames isolating the horror in his daughter's eyes, squeezing away the young woman who had no doubt furnished his only pleasure, his only redemption, and his only currency for a recounting of the past, a remeasuring in terms of the golden skin exposed to the sunset that produced shapes of what his wife had been; and traces of what, the detective sergeant mused, he may have held himself to have been—thus the brutalizer brutalized in his own coin? No doubt, but could it be transmitted to Mr. Bates? They were two fathers—he himself of course in every sense except the literal one—they could join together.

The young woman's cries must have broken like wet bamboo as the dying body continued to eye her, blinked perhaps, spilling tears, reading the outlines of her naked form like sentences falling into the trough of death, while the other members of the event approached from their two directions, stretched, watching, two strings about to snap.

"Plo-xlong killed him, shot him in the back. Didn't he?"

"No."

"Don't say anything," Mr. Bates croaked.

"He was hiding in the bushes. He waited until you walked up the beach, then opened fire."

"I killed him."

Philip looked down at his hands. Well, the policeman sighed. A long way to go. He settled back again, his chin sunk onto his chest. No one helped him. He had to do everything by himself. Yet wasn't there always room for forgiveness? He observed the son, slumped in hostility. There would be clemency for him, and for his father, too.

The policeman tried to feel better. Wouldn't his heart spread open wide enough to accept even the rogue geologist? He gazed up at the wet green lips of overhanging trees. Of course it would. He was at bottom soft, moist, a deep pool—particularly now that his rival was dead. Didn't he have more room to move? Yes. You drink from me too, he thought toward his new ghost, and felt himself flood with pleasure. This was a wonderful world; tongues, lips: things happened on their own. Yes. He experienced a rush of self-consciousness and stared into his police cap.

Nothing. He glanced around. Neither of them was

watching him. Well, then, Mr. Bates would be missing it
all, so concerned was he with the hunched and bitter
prisoner—fruit of his seed stained here the color of stagnant water. The policeman ran his tongue along the scars
on the back of his fist. Only he, only the senior officer who
had held himself upright, who had remained whole, celi-
bate, and who had thus developed powers of reflection
beyond those of others; only he had learned that one
acted on the world, one waded in, one became involved,
made one's arrests with firmness and compassion, and
indulged and indulged and indulged until the indulgee
was packed into himself like so many numbers waiting
only to be counted, flicked open—insides glassy as beads.

No, he affirmed, we weren't so much alone as, as . . .
what? He'd lost the thread. He fitted his teeth at either
edge of the main ridge of scar tissue running down his
knuckles. Why couldn't they talk to each other? The son
was sunk on one side, the father lost on the other. Why
were they so far apart?

He thought of his brother. Would Plo-xlong try to shift
his crime onto Mr. Bates's son? That would contain a
measure of failure, but he might believe that he had no
choice.

What was love, then, if not a willingness to give the
other room to surrender? To draw the perimeter wide
enough to allow the wallower wallowing space? Yes!
Leniency, pure and simple, and of course the ability to
be at the right place at the right time with the right response. Yes! He sucked at his fist. Yes, and the capacity
to deliver the response. Yes, and, and, and, what? Moule

said? Human affection? Fine, sure, no problem there, largely true, given the, the, the various constraints involved in dealing with the, the, the . . .

Something was definitely wrong. He paused in his musings. Was he slurping? Someone was. One did one's best and took one's lumps and . . .

No one helped him. He wanted to explain that he wasn't unaware of the perplexity of the father and son also trapped in this moment at this table. They were both staring at him now, paying a lot of attention to him now. Was he making that noise? Why were his fingers in his mouth? With the application of a tremendous amount of willpower, he managed to extract his hand and examine it. It was pink and shiny from sucking. Lonely, lonely. Was something wrong? But what? He wanted to explain that there was always something else, something electric in the wet air just beyond his grasp, something elusive.

He tried to stand; his feet were numb. It was another attack. How had he failed to see it coming? He strained to focus his attention. Out here it could be dangerous.

The father had grown as pale as the son. They were talking to each other, but the words were lost in the ringing bangs of bells in his ears.

His men squatted in a circle, feeding on something one of them had snared. They were either hungry, or sleepy, or ruttish. It was hard to imagine how any of them could ever be developed into an officer of the law.

Mr. Bates seemed to be moving directly toward him. Was the man speaking to him?

He would have liked to join his men and open up

a reconstruction of the crime—one of the moments of police work he found most satisfying, filled, as it always was, with telling—explanations, speculations, diagrams scratched in the mud—anything could be brought to life if one attached the right words to it.

What was Mr. Bates doing? Why had he left the table?

He would have enjoyed squatting among them, crowing over the shoot-out on the riverbank, pawing over the pair of dead rebels, fingering the captured tin. Why did he always hesitate? Lonely, lonely. Was he afraid to release the distance required to control them? Perhaps, but he was far from them, too far, and with no real hope of crossing back. He stared into the tree above him. Down the tunnel of a single leaf he could see explosions, flames leaping up through the splintered longhouse, the geologist posing calmly at the edge of the clearing; and himself too, removed, observing.

His junior officer now stood beside the elder foreigner. Was he being spoken to? So it seemed. His concentration was at the moment a shade too fine. He was somewhere else. Was he to be picked up? But one's senior officer wasn't to be touched! Was he to be placed in the shade? This happened, this happened, he knew this happened. He would be back.

The junior officer brought bottles of beer for the two foreigners. The younger had nothing to be ashamed of. He had lingered with the corpse as long as he dared, protecting what he would claim to have killed against the threat of marauding scavengers. Terror at the night jungle had finally sent him scrambling along the moonlit edge of the river, stumbling over exposed roots and splashing up silver fans of spray from stagnant pools.

Two of the militiamen began squabbling over a piece of flesh. The junior officer didn't seem to notice. He should have turned at once and distracted them. Such was the duty of the man in command.

The detective sergeant's eyes found his fingers. He saw the shape of his younger brother, crouched in the shadows of yesterday's roadside trees and ticking with vengeance, his palm perfectly suited to the notched grip of his pistol.

"I'm guilty!"

Detective Sergeant Xlong drifted to the surface for a moment. The younger foreigner, still shackled to the table leg, had stood—hunched forward, leaning over the table and glaring at his father. He wavered, the father wavered; then the policeman noticed the whole world was wavering, so he settled back into the steaming shade of his strangler fig. The pungent bark reminded him of his mother. Could he go there? To the river? To where she was dead? She would be proud of her middle son.

He saw the sunlight of yesterday's grove in the greasy sheen of his thumbnails. He sensed the brown breasts of his niece slick with river water, the crunch of Philip's anger as he stalked off up the beach, filled with disgust at his would-be father-in-law.

He called toward his knuckles, and heard the trees shudder at the shadow bent with hatred, heard his younger brother creeping forward, already well within range. He tasted the acid in his brother's throat as he swallowed to still his heart further—a single step from stopping it altogether. He tasted his brother's pain as he sought his target down the corridor of his rage, confined, confined, seating the nipple in its notch and climbing down the lonely blued barrel to the swollen mound of his enemy.

The detective sergeant, gliding in a green net of flies, heard the name of their elder brother whispered as the first hole of blood bloomed in the dirty white shirt, heard the name repeated with each slap of the garden until the clip was empty and the action no longer kicked against the assassin's thumb.

The policeman realized he was regaining control of his hands. He turned his head. His neck was stiff, but he had articulation. He watched the pair at the table— the son: querulous, bitter; the father: silent now, offering no response.

The policeman's heart again filled with compassion. They were his, his alone. The blank amazement on the face of his junior officer offered proof that he himself would never be replaced. Only he fully accepted the terrible burden of life in the police.

Yes, he could appreciate Philip's regret at abandoning the corpse of the father of the young woman with whom he had fallen in love. Acts of civic responsibility in the male were pivotal to the successful manipulation of a romance, he thought, recognizing in his syntax the return to health. He smiled. His young prisoner obviously retained a touch of the lover, clinging like the hint of metal in a freshly opened tin of sardines.

Yes. Detective Sergeant Xlong's fingers plucked at the mud banked against the lateral surface root beside him. He had been tested. He squeezed the dark earth into his fist, forcing three wet tongues out between his fingers to form in mud the triangle he had suspected from the beginning—his niece bent in confusion over her dying father, glaring fearfully at the face of Plo-xlong; his younger brother, amazed by the fact that it had been brought home at last; and Berthe again, turning with one final appeal to the third member of the event: the foreigner with his feet in the wet sand, a loaded pistol in his hand and no reason now not to do something—except . . . what? The policeman hung up on the boy's motive. It must have been because he detected the lips and cheekbones of Berthe within the face of Plo-xlong that he hesitated, thus setting up the situation which would lead to his own near death.

The policeman studied his slumped prisoner. He hoped it wasn't just love. He tossed the three mud lumps aside. The investigation was gummed up enough as it was.

His eyes focused easily now. He licked his lips, aware of sensation. The father had begun talking rapidly, chopping the air with the blade of his hand, outlining, explaining, pleading, demanding.

"You could have shot him," the policeman said from the shade of his tree. "Shot him, and thrown the pistol into the river."

Philip didn't bother to repeat his confession.

"No," the policeman continued. "I meant Plo-xlong. But you didn't shoot the other one, either."

George Bates gazed at him in outrage, but Philip's face was calm for the first time since his capture.

Detective Sergeant Xlong suddenly realized there was a deeper connection between Philip and his younger brother than he had expected.

"You knew him? You had seen him before?"

Philip smiled at the policeman's recognition. He still didn't say anything.

◆❪❬◆❪❬◆❪❬◆❪❬◆❪❬◆❪❬◆❪❬

"Can't you see you've got to stop that? He's trying to trap you!"

Detective Sergeant Xlong glanced at the pair behind him. Philip's face had curled with irony. He asked if his father believed he wasn't trapped already.

"We'll work something out."

The boy's eyes met those of the policeman, then dropped away. He shrugged. His father could do whatever he wanted.

The soldier marching in front of Detective Sergeant Xlong began splashing up mud. "Farther forward," the policeman ordered. The fellow didn't respond; he must have fallen asleep again. "Maintain an interval." He knew they made too good a target when bunched together.

Could Philip truly be so indifferent to his fate? The policeman was tempted to grant as much, for the boy seemed to believe he had been trapped all his life. If so, then wouldn't his duty be—as professional policeman and thus ranking expert in these affairs—to offer a measure of relief? Punch out a quick dosage of hope? Something, say, in a rigorous interpretation of the illusory nature of freedom? Wouldn't that help the boy up out of his hole?

Hard to say. Philosophy here was a lot like eating an eel: once you got into it, you never knew exactly where you were. The detective sergeant smiled ruefully; speculation often made him lonely.

Philip had stayed with the corpse until darkness flowing out of the river had filled him with dread. The night jungle must seem unbearable to a foreigner. He would become frightened by the stifling lightlessness under the canopy. Even the rogue geologist had refused to venture outside at night, particularly when he was older and less mobile. The policeman had never understood his fear. The man had ears, didn't he? Fingertips, tongue, why couldn't he learn to adapt?

Philip had waited with the corpse because he thought Berthe might send someone to help him. He hadn't guessed that she had fled all the way downriver to her uncle. She must have believed he was the only man who could save him.

The young foreigner had splashed upriver as far as a trail that connected to the temple he had once visited with Berthe. At that familiar sight, he had begun to feel slightly reassured. He entered the black path cautiously, his hands feeling before him, tense for any shift in the darkness. At the end of the tunnel of trees, moonlight flooded the clearing; and despite his anxiety, the ruins appeared as splendid as anything he had ever seen. The silvery stone walls shivered like wet sheets of cream, and the pockets of shadows seemed velvet with life.

Philip told how he had passed through each of the front galleries, peering into the empty chambers before daring to cross them. Shattered statues the color of smoke floated above the black stones of the floor. The faces of meditating deities had been so disfigured by ages of lichens and rain that visages which had once guaranteed serenity now only showed the process of decay.

Philip had arrived near the center of the temple when he experienced a sensation of gradual sinking. He stooped to feel the earth; it was solid. He glanced up; the moon was racing against thickening clouds. He realized then he would soon be plunged into total darkness. He had to continue. From the far side of the back portico he knew he could find the road that led to the smeltery. By that time he had even begun to sense that he wasn't alone, yet he didn't dare abandon the only landmark in the area.

The detective sergeant had been told how Philip felt his way among the maze of walls, straining to pick up any sound of danger. The boy had moved slowly; patches of deeper blackness could indicate either an open passageway or a blank wall. Philip said his concentration had been so intense, so perfect, that he had almost reached the outermost portico of the compound before he was captured.

It was as if the rebels had arrived in layers. At first there was nothing more than a sour impatience permeating the air, a sense of dissatisfaction so fundamental it must have been acquired at birth. Philip had continued forward, halting more frequently as the surrounding darkness filled with a malevolent odor of urine and decayed leather. His movements grew increasingly hesitant until at some point he recognized that he had become motionless, frozen by the taste of a gathering purpose in the night air. He couldn't recall when he had first sensed the dull glint of tin. The exposure of the metal to the last of the moonlight chilled him, although he wasn't sure if he had actually seen the stolen tin or simply felt it along his skin, clinging to him like a greasy curd; but he did know that he was about to face his moment within the hands of the abandoned; and he was afraid. The rebels must have assembled and ripped open one of the sacks, unable to restrain their longing to gloat over booty. Invisible to the boy, as random as ants, they sighed as they glided along the worn stone porches.

Philip had fitted himself into a dark section of wall. He could detect certain quarters of the blackness which were more tangible. He released his breath shallowly. His only hope was to remain soundless. He waited.

At one point, a pair of shadows drifted so near to where he was hiding that he could have touched them. They were two patches of heat, two columns of musk. The only sound was the occasional shudder of an automatic rifle brushed against an outcropping of stone. They passed beyond his niche, feeling their way toward the path that led to the river.

Some sought perches above him, settling into broken towers and folding down their elbows and knees, smoothing their clothing and cushioning their rifles against meaty pads. Others still drifted along the surface of the portico flooring, sliding easily, their movements tuned to each other, their heads no doubt all facing the same way, mouths slowly reaching out for wet gulps of night air.

He was being encircled; there was no question. He still tried to listen for any sign, but the blood now beating in his ears distracted him. Once again one crossed so closely above him that the gray breath of the smuggler's unwashed clothing flowed down over his cheeks and ears, filling his mouth with fear and tensing his neck against the hooked fingers that hadn't quite detected him.

Nothing happened. The man passed. They were spreading throughout the ruins, suspending themselves in a pattern none of them could have explained, but one that must inevitably produce a capture. Did they know what they were drawing toward? Philip wondered if they had perhaps been hoping for food. He said that at the moment he had accepted that he would be killed, he had also realized that his fear at that fact wasn't necessarily less pointless than the rebels' pathetic pleasure in their sacks of raw tin.

Perhaps, the policeman had smiled. But that hadn't made the boy any less grateful for the bursts of automatic rifle fire that freed him, for the two squads charging from opposite sides, for the militiamen selected for the sole task of preventing his guards from slitting his throat. Wasn't that so?

Philip hadn't answered, and the policeman had let the silence stand. He had wondered if Mr. Bates would also realize that patience was called for. Unfortunately, he had had ample evidence to the contrary.

No, the detective sergeant agreed with himself, detaining one of his militiamen in order to tighten the damp leather straps that crossed the man's back. Mr. Bates could not understand. Nor was Philip's execution simply to have been an arbitrary bit of revolutionary justice. Despite what must have seemed overwhelming provocation, Plo-xlong had never developed into much of a shooter. If nothing else, the geologist's embarrassing longevity was proof of this. Poor Plo-xlong. His initial failure at assassination had probably fouled his self-confidence. No doubt his brother might have considered Philip a possible rival, but that in itself wouldn't have been enough. The policeman gazed at the boy who was slogging along, handcuffed to a militiaman. He was obviously withholding information. He would need a little room before he could unburden himself, that much was clear. The appropriate police technique would center on the firm application of an absence.

Detective Sergeant Xlong sighed to think of the complexity before him. How simple his boyhood seemed in comparison. Even after the death of Fing, he had still found his basic nurturing in the steamy gloom of the jungle. Only at the arrival of the rogue geologist had the world bloomed open for him, dazzling him with its seething variety.

On the afternoon of the arrival, every member of the kampong had gathered in front of the longhouse. They had waited under the sun, dressed in their finery. The middle brother proudly had on his pants—at that time the only pair remaining. He assumed the geologist would recognize his uniqueness. He had gradually become an outcast, but he felt then that his weeks of loneliness might be at an end. He stood in front. He sensed his destiny, and he prepared for the breach.

As the nuptial canoes had rounded the bend and headed toward the docking bank, Plo-xlong began his attack. He drifted back behind the crowd to retrieve his weapons. No one noticed him. He returned with the bow and arrow held casually against his side. He was calm and deliberate. He worked his way into the crowd. The paddlers struggled to hold the canoe sideways against the current. The geologist stood, a tall and golden target in the afternoon light.

Plo-xlong sprinted to the water's edge. Still no one noticed him. Pumped up with rage, standing at near point-blank range, he notched his arrow and drew it all the way to his chest. He shouted once. The bowstring snapped. The arrow wobbled hopelessly on his fist for a moment, then dropped into the water. It was caught by the current and drifted away.

If the advancing bridegroom saw the insult, he made no indication. The sunlight glittered on his golden head more brightly than on the face of the river. He did nothing. His paddlers continued battling against the side wash, trying to force the canoe with its awkward upright burden nose first into the green mud of the landing. The geologist had insisted upon stepping directly onto the shore.

With a howl of disappointment, the youngest brother threw down his useless bow and fled into the jungle. From that day he was known as Plo-xlong, the term "Plo" being their word for the active, fiery element in the traditional Chinese yin-yang pair of opposites.

Mr. Bates had begun to berate his son again. The boy was sick; why didn't he leave him alone? Detective Sergeant Xlong considered distracting the father with an explanation of his younger brother's name. Would Mr. Bates see that as a gesture of reconciliation between them? Would he accept a role in a dialogue and inquire after the word for the female principle?

The policeman turned back toward the pair behind him. The father continued to batter against what he saw as his son's sullenness. "Prajaengluengloeung," the policeman repeated to himself, settling for his own pleasure in the word. Mr. Bates would probably make some negative comment. He would miss the inscrutability of the female implied by the term and thus be unable to appreciate how the policeman had always found his most satisfying carnal release in language.

But would that matter? How had he allowed the elder foreigner to assume such a role of dominance? He himself had grown too cautious. The investigation might suffer.

He had tried to discuss his theory of the language of love with Moule, but she grew impatient with words. He recalled how once he had attempted to describe her to herself in terms of patches of color, squinting in order to facilitate the necessary blur. "That's pink, that's taupe, that's tan, that's black"—she had not been pleased.

Love, he thought, scratching his neck as a test for sensation. It was not his natural stamping ground. Once he had explained to Moule how love could be like when something died under your house. Although you could forget about it as long as you kept busy, relax a bit and there it was: a curious, steady pressure on the nose; asking the hard question, turning your attention willy-nilly toward the strings of your groin—whoosh! What a distraction: sprouting like hair from the weather, and yet somehow just not quite troublesome enough to make you want to get down and crawl under and drag it out.

Moule had just stared at him. He had asked her what she thought. She shook her head. Maybe they each ought to be seeing other people. That was not what he had expected. It was a shame Moule didn't always appreciate his explanations.

Still, "prajaengluengloeung" was beautiful—and easier to deal with, too. He wasn't quite ready to abandon emotion completely.

That day the lead canoe had beached and the geologist had stepped ashore. The middle brother had kicked the bow into the river. There would be no advantage for anyone to know that the string had been partially severed. The geologist examined the group on the mud bank, perhaps searching for his bride. She had modestly hidden herself. The insides of her thighs were swollen with the lizard infections of her nuptial tattoos.

The rogue geologist had continued to wait, his shoes sinking into the soft green mud. None of the other canoes would land until he moved up toward the longhouse to salute the clan's ancestor pole. It had been hung with a fresh pair of pig heads in celebration of the event.

Should the headman have led him through a ceremony? Nothing like his arrival had ever happened; no practice seemed appropriate. They hadn't known what to do, so they had done nothing. The bridegroom had stood gazing at the pole. He must have realized that it was up to him to introduce the proper format. He unholstered his black pistol and attached it to the base of the pole, binding it on with strips of wet skin. He stepped back and, raising his right hand, shouted some sort of pledge in his native English. No one understood much of it. It seemed to be a mass of irrelevant promises; yet when he finished, it was as if a covenant had been set. They had been irrevocably bound. The pistol made an awesome seal—not even cheapened when they realized he had others, lots of others. The original held a promise they continued to acknowledge even during the darkest periods of his disintegration.

Detective Sergeant Xlong measured his people's modern history from that moment when the geologist had secured his pistol to their ancestor totem. He had known intuitively that nothing would ever be the same again. It was a lesson he had had little chance to forget. The dead packed in his shoulders had made sure of that.

Mr. Bates demanded to know why anyone would want to kill Philip. The boy hadn't done anything. He wasn't involved.

Philip shook his head. His attention had again turned toward Detective Sergeant Xlong. Was he searching his face too for some shadow of family resemblance? The policeman felt the investigation wandering out of control. He slapped both palms against his cheeks to stir himself.

"I'm guilty," Philip insisted, obviously willing to make demands on the policeman.

"You didn't do anything!" his father shouted. "Nothing's wrong."

"Nothing," Philip echoed. He wavered momentarily, as if he had detected a measure of redemption in his father's appeal. "Sins of omission, then."

"But you didn't kill anybody!"

"But I did."

Detective Sergeant Xlong raised his hand. He would take a moment to reassure Mr. Bates. There were inconsistencies in his son's position. There would be other interrogations, other opportunities for arrangement. Mr.

Bates might find comfort in the notion that everything was in flux—with the necessary exception, of course, of the basic forms of police behavior.

Clearly, an investigation was the responsibility of the senior members of the force; yet the concerned citizen—the concerned guest, rather—could also play a useful role.

"You think I don't know what you're up to? You think I haven't been onto you since the day I arrived?"

Well, there was no cause for blame. George Bates might restore his former calm through the mediation of a conundrum: moral culpability here was not dissimilar from soup. Every day one tossed in scraps, and every day one drained off a meal. Thus, although the consistency was never the same, one always knew what to call it.

Mr. Bates stared at him for a moment without speaking, then abruptly turned his back—a gesture with which the policeman had become thoroughly familiar.

Detective Sergeant Xlong ordered his men into motion. It was time to pick up the pace. George Bates, despite the ground he had lost, was to take heart. The nature of the event could be couched in the vocabulary of the police, without whose steadying gaze, it could be argued, the crime itself would cease to exist. The force was what obtained. This, the detective sergeant insisted, would be his final message. Everything was under control.

Mr. Bates shook his head. Philip's lips had curved into an odd smile. His guard urged him forward. He didn't move.

"I was in your longhouse," the boy said, "the night before the murder."

Yes, well, it was time to go. Most things were under

control. And, and, and everything changed, including the police—no, rather, excepting the police, as they were by definition always the same.

"I saw your sister, and your brother."

Yes, well, what wasn't the same was what was changing and, could be said to be what . . .

"Can you guess what they were doing?"

. . . what was permanent; change, that is.

"Shall I tell you?"

No. He raised his hand. This was hardly the time. Leaves, water, weather, and the reliability of automatic weapons—one clutched at what one knew. "Back to town!" the policeman shouted. Monkeys howled, birds screamed, the entire jungle gathered together to hoot at the column of men on their way, the policeman recognized, to one jail or another.

◆(◆(◆(◆(◆(◆(◆(◆(◆(◆(

"You, sir, are the arresting officer?"

The policeman cracked his knuckles and smiled. He was pleased by the judge's ceremony. The man's clothing seemed fresh, his face was washed. Obviously he was determined not to disgrace local jurisprudence before their foreign guests.

Detective Sergeant Xlong came to his feet as slowly as possible. Everyone was watching him. He regretted that the arraignment would not be more taxing. His Honor the judge might have revealed new qualities of strength had he been required to attend to a more ambitious strategy.

"I am, Your Honor."

"And you are prepared to charge this Mr. Bates Philip with the crime of . . . ?"

"Bates comma Philip, Your Honor."

"That's right. So, this Mr. Philip Bates, then, with the crime of murder?"

The detective sergeant didn't answer. He had breakfasted with the judge and explained how the case was to be handled. He always felt most comfortable with the arraignment process itself. The malefactor's name passed through the public's jaws. The stress was on counting, on forming lists, on days and dates and probable causes. Unanticipated bits of information dropped into the case like juice from wounded birds, and duty itself seemed most rewarding.

Later, the dead fingers of the code would clog up the sweep of the production. Once the prosecuting attorney got his teeth into it, once the defense attorney began spreading his gas, there would be no end to the confusion; and the streamlined shape the policeman had been at such pains to provide would become so swollen with the waste products of the adversary mode that he could hardly bear to follow the proceedings, so much had it become like the corruption of one's child.

"Detective Sergeant?"

"I haven't been sworn in yet, Your Honor."

On his way to the arraignment hearing, Detective Sergeant Xlong had discovered the prosecuting attorney waist-deep in rotting old law books, his clothes soaked and his eyes pinched with gloom as he copied out archaic phrases from laws that had been forced to the surface after decades underwater. He, too, was obviously stimulated by the prospect of a foreigner in the dock. The policeman had passed on silently. He hadn't told him his labor would be fruitless.

"Call Berthe Xlong."

Philip jumped to his feet. He didn't want her involved. His father reached for his arm, but the boy pushed past him. He demanded to take the stand himself.

The prosecutor lifted his face from the papers spread along the table. His nostrils flared; he scented an irregularity. This was his chance to strike. He stood to make a motion, but the judge knew better than to recognize him. Philip continued to approach the bench. The prosecutor followed him, one arm beating against his thigh like a broken wing.

Detective Sergeant Xlong tugged his cap more tightly down over his eyes. That boy was a disaster. Was it too late to signal for an adjournment? He tilted his head back to see. Philip was already on the stand, his hand up, being sworn. The policeman sensed his case falling apart. He hunched down into his seat. Nobody helped him.

The judge questioned Philip himself. The boy demanded to be allowed to confess, but the judge maintained control of the proceedings. What did Philip claim to have killed the geologist with? A pistol. Where did he get this pistol? The geologist gave it to him. Why did he do that?

"He wanted me to shoot someone. The smeltery had almost completely collapsed. No one did any work. There hadn't been any production for months. He wanted me to help him get the business started again."

"Who did he want you to shoot?"

"Plo-xlong. He said if we killed Plo-xlong, the rebels would come back to the smeltery."

"Did you believe that?"

Philip shook his head. Of course not.

"So you refused to take part in the assassination?"

"No, I didn't refuse."

The judge stared at him for a moment. Hadn't he just said he believed such an act would have no effect?

Philip suddenly seemed reticent. He looked at his feet.

He hadn't refused, yet he hadn't done it either. Wasn't that correct?

It was. But there was more to it.

The judge glanced at the policeman. This was not what he had expected. Detective Sergeant Xlong shrugged. They might as well go along with whatever was coming.

"When was this assassination to take place?"

"The night before . . ."

"Before what?"

"Before I killed the geologist on the riverbank."

"Your Honor!" George Bates jumped to his feet. "Listen, he's upset. He didn't kill anyone!"

Philip glared at his father. "That's not for you to decide," he shouted.

The judge rapped his gavel, but Mr. Bates turned toward Detective Sergeant Xlong. "You know he's not guilty. Why don't you say something?"

"Bad water," the policeman began, "and bad food, lack of sleep, various viral infections; as you know, the inner ear is particularly . . ."

"Damn!" Mr. Bates cried. "He's not guilty!"

The policeman suggested that Mr. Bates was blinded by his desire to protect his son from punishment.

"He's trying to goad you. He wants to pay for something he didn't do."

"Why?"

Mr. Bates remained standing, staring down at the policeman. He thrust his hands into his pockets, but the answer to Detective Sergeant Xlong's question seemed beyond him. The policeman and the judge observed each other solemnly. The arraignment had become a shambles. Even the prosecuting attorney was now pleading some sort of brief, flapping his arms in the air and wiping his lips on his sleeve. It was time to cut losses.

Philip was conducted into the judge's chambers. His father tried to follow but the policeman refused. Guards were posted. The prisoner's privacy would be respected.

The judge perched on the edge of his musty chair. His eyes were bright; he was enjoying himself. He shuffled some papers on his desk but neither Philip nor the policeman paid any attention to him.

"Your father seems upset."

Philip smiled.

"You don't think you could make things easier on him?"

"And on you?"

"And on all of us?"

The boy shrugged.

"And on Berthe, too?"

"She's not in this."

"Her father is—was, rather. You don't think she feels it?"

"She hated him."

"No doubt. We all did. But she's still his daughter."

"He was never a real father to her."

"Nevertheless, she . . ."

"Why don't you say what's really on your mind? It's not Berthe you're worried about."

"Worried? We of the police rarely worry."

"Sure."

The policeman removed his cap and studied the sweatband. He plucked at the gray salt crust formed at the base of the visor.

"You want to know about your brother, don't you?"

Detective Sergeant Xlong glanced at Philip but didn't answer.

"You know I could've killed him," the boy said. It was almost a plea.

"Why didn't you?"

Philip stared at the policeman for a moment, then lowered his eyes. That was what he'd been asking himself. He hadn't come up with an answer. At first he thought he'd simply been in the jungle so long that he'd lost touch with the outside world, but that wasn't it. He'd known what was happening and hadn't believed a word the geologist told him. They used to sit on the screened veranda as evening settled into the jungle. The geologist was so bloated that he could scarcely walk. He might have been taunting his enemies, presenting a target boldly dressed in a dirty white suit and daring them to try to assassinate him. He glared at the blank face of the night jungle and steadily fed out of a tin basin of food. He tried to explain himself to the boy. Berthe stood behind her father with a wet towel to wipe grease from his lips and a pair of long bamboo tweezers in case his trachea became clogged.

Philip had pretended to follow his explanations, but it was the chill in his own heart that concerned him. He had confessed his sense of failure and the geologist had nodded, his mouth too full to comment. Sometimes the man's throat would become so constricted with fever that he could barely swallow. He would continue chewing, extracting what he could from his food before spitting back the fiber, the gristle, the bones, seeds, rinds, shells, whatever couldn't be swallowed. At such times only Philip would still be able to talk, filling the heavy wet air with his sense of dread while the geologist puffed out his cheeks and chewed.

Philip had discovered that he needed to live on the edge of the world if he was to live at all, and nothing seemed more firmly there than the smeltery. It was the one place where he felt he could directly face the blades he sensed hanging over him. On the night before the murder, Philip had had the clearest sense of his fear. It was when he confessed that he needed to confront this demon that the geologist produced the pistol. The man's fever had been particularly bad all day. Even with the usual remission at evening, there was a real danger of strangulation, so he said very little.

They had sat together, aware of the possible harmony between them. Because Philip had recognized only that he could no longer merely be a tourist, he still had little response to what the geologist was suggesting. The man spoke carefully, his words garbled by the mouthful of chewed food. He explained how to use the rebels. They shouldn't be destroyed. Enemies were a source of profits. Competition was a sign of healthy commerce—provided one maintained the essential degree of control. He explained how to detect the strings of the economy. He explained how to release commodities, how to flood markets, how to underprice. He explained how to gauge the degree of loyalty necessary for production and how to blend it with a healthy dose of superstitious fear.

The geologist's teeth were worn down as flat as river pebbles, but he attempted the rib cage of a jungle bird without hesitation. He needed an heir. He was like a father bribing a stranger to take on his pregnant daughter, although the fact that he actually had a daughter seemed scarcely relevant. He never mentioned Berthe, not until the next day. It was the smeltery that he wanted to transmit; that was his only concern. "Kill Plo-xlong," he said, bird bones protruding from the corners of his mouth, "and the others will follow you." Philip knew there would be no use in trying to disagree.

They had sat up waiting into the depths of the night, the pistol and the tin basin of food between them. At last the geologist's jaws sagged open and Philip knew he had fallen asleep. Berthe bent over her father to clear the remaining food from his mouth; and as she did so, her eyes met Philip's. He watched her stretch down the loose flesh of her father's cheeks with a flat spatula and methodically work the dross from the back of his mouth toward the front. He suddenly had an urge to seize her, to crush her in his arms, to feel her heart beating behind her breasts; but he hesitated, knowing that he was missing his chance but unable to move. In the end he could do nothing more than pry down her father's lower lip while she scraped out the vegetable fibers packed under his tongue.

"Love," the policeman said sympathetically. He'd never had much luck with it either.

Philip hung his head. He'd snatched up the pistol and run into the jungle. Berthe had followed him, telling him that it didn't matter. He couldn't explain what he'd wanted to happen. He'd certainly had no intention of fighting for the smeltery. He hadn't felt that he was so much on his way to try to kill Plo-xlong as he was on his way to see what it might feel like if he should decide to try later.

The policeman scratched his ear. "You mean you were practicing?"

No, it wasn't so much a rehearsal as a test. How could he know if he could do something unless he knew what it might feel like to be able to do it?

"You were playing?"

Philip nodded. That wasn't it exactly, but it was a kind of manipulation. Even at the moment of confrontation, he'd understood that the closest he could come to being alive was to mimic the forms of the living.

The policeman didn't understand.

"My life is a mockery," Philip said calmly. The only thing that was out of character was that he'd failed to get lost on his way to the longhouse. It would have been more typical of him to have wandered in circles, or maybe to have broken his leg.

"Or to have lost the pistol on the way, or to have forgotten to load it."

The policeman again couldn't understand. Did he mean he wanted to fail?

"Of course. Subconsciously, that was probably exactly what I wanted."

"But you didn't?"

No. He had found the longhouse. He'd only seen it from the river, yet he never left the correct path. He said it was as if he had been guided. The jungle was pitch black; it should have been impossible to negotiate the entire distance. He never made a mistake. He stumbled into the support poles of the longhouse before he realized he'd arrived.

He had stopped, his heart pounding. He could smell the dirty yellow foam on the river and the garbage rotting under the building, but he still couldn't see it.

"I mean I could smell the yellowness, you know?"

Every odor became pronounced—oil from the pistol, sweat in his clothing, the mold covering the bottom supports of the old bamboo building. The muffled wetness of the jungle still seemed to roar down over him; but because he couldn't see, he felt betrayed.

"Betrayed? By what?"

He had almost turned to go back. He was finished. Then he happened to look up. The longhouse hung above him like a huge black fish cruising through the night sky, blanking out the stars. He had the sudden notion it was about to swallow him. Every moment of his life was packed into that single, swollen, immense black fish. He understood that what he had to do was kill it.

He crept up the notched log. He had the sensation of being slightly ahead of himself in time. It was as if he had already done it, or had done it all once before and was now simply retracing it. There were no transitions. He was on the notched log, then he was in the shadows of a bamboo lattice, pointing his pistol at the two people wrapped in each other's arms beside the low fire.

"You didn't shoot."

He smiled. It was as if he had been afraid of the noise. There was a little light there; the room was silent and the noise would have been awful. He didn't want to scare them.

"But you were going to kill them?"

"Yes. I suppose. . . . But I didn't want to *scare* them. Can't you understand?"

The detective sergeant and the judge looked at each other. Thank God the prosecuting attorney had been barred. What a mess *he* would have made out of such testimony. The detective sergeant's intuition had been correct. The boy was dangerous—although not in the way he'd thought.

Philip told how the pair had sensed his presence at the same instant he'd realized he wouldn't be able to shoot them. They looked up at him, both at the same time, their faces mild and unafraid. He had thought that they were lovers, but the woman was a lot older. She was holding the man's head against her chest and tucking strands of hair behind his ears.

"Why did you say that before? About what they were doing?"

Philip looked at his hands. He almost seemed not to remember the remark.

"I mean about Plo-xlong and my sister—our sister, I mean?"

"Because I was lonely," Philip cried suddenly. "Because seeing them made me so damn lonely I wanted to blot it out!"

The policeman stood up. He cracked his knuckles and straightened his cap. This was a good world, he thought. Things were in order.

Philip had stared at the couple in the firelight, almost mesmerized by their lack of panic. He stood in the shadows, pointing the gun at them, unable to move. The man didn't try to rise. He looked at the boy, looked at the gun, but his head hardly lifted from the woman's chest.

Philip said he became filled with an odd rage. They were too peaceful. Again, it dropped on him like a wave that every moment of his life had been collected up into this chance—and that the only possible realization would begin with the shooting of Plo-xlong. The room was silent. The low fire burned with a slow cold flame. Had Plo-xlong stirred, had he said a word, Philip was sure he would have emptied the pistol into him. But the man just continued staring at him, waiting for the explosions. Then, at some moment they both recognized as the point at which it should happen, he closed his eyes and, turning his cheek back down against the woman, gradually pulled his knees up against his belly as if he wanted to sleep.

Philip had cocked back the hammer. He knew there was nothing left but to do it. Holding the pistol was like clasping an open mouth in his fist. But he had also realized he was already only waiting for the trigger to suck his finger home. The gesture was empty. He had surrendered the moment.

"So you still didn't shoot?"

No. Because what he'd wanted was for the woman to hold him the way she was holding Plo-xlong.

Fine, the policeman thought. Things certainly were in order. He had been correct. Here was no killer. The arraignment hearing could resume. He might even allow the boy to be bound over for trial. Why not toss a bone to the judicial system? They would enjoy having something complicated to suck on. His Honor here would salivate at the prospect. The whole group might see it as a chance for a jurisprudence renaissance, and they could be trusted to appreciate its source.

He adjusted his cap again. It never seemed quite right. Of course, on the other hand, that would mean that he too would have to be involved. He thought of all those hours spent in the musty company of lawyers and knew he'd never permit it. He had wasted enough afternoons in the past watching pairs of them attempting to web each other into one legal corner or another. No, better to be back with his men, regulating the flow of food. One knew where one belonged.

Philip told how he must have been in the longhouse for hours. He had backed deeper into the shadows, still watching. They knew he hadn't left; there was nothing they could do. He thought Plo-xlong might have actually gone to sleep, he was so motionless. The woman never took her eyes off the dark patch where he was hiding. He could read her bitterness, her fear, and, most unnerving, her terrible submissiveness. She made no move to approach him; but he felt himself washed in her eyes, twisted and stretched in them as if he were not so much human as a natural force of pure malevolence. He had been stripped. His whole life had been channeled through her eyes; and when at last he left, he knew nothing would ever be the same.

By the time he retreated down the notched log, it was almost light enough to see. The river and trees were still black; but the sky was gray, and the monkeys were all awake, laughing and yelling at him. He passed into their hooting chatter, convinced that it was no worse than he deserved.

"You're no killer."

Philip didn't remember much from that morning. He had returned to the smeltery. There wasn't much he could say; he wandered around aimlessly, certain everyone was waiting for him to decide what he was going to do next. It was like standing poised on the edge of a diving board, staring at the water, not so much afraid of the dive as simply unable to work up sufficient energy to begin it.

Finally, late in the afternoon, the three of them had made their way down to the bathing shallows. They were aware that they were running out of time. The truce they'd established could never be any more than temporary. It was up to Philip to indicate the direction—and he still hesitated. Each was alone, wrapped in a shell of self-consciousness. The geologist had mentioned nothing of the night before. Perhaps he assumed that whatever had happened would have to work out to his benefit.

Berthe had walked a few feet ahead of the other two, carrying her soap and shampoo and scrubbing pumice in a plastic pail. Philip knew that her attitude toward him had shifted, but he wasn't sure in exactly what way. She seemed cooler, more formal, and at the same time deeply conscious of the fact that a new connection had been established between them. The night before she had cried that he was abandoning her in the same way her father had abandoned her mother. He'd wanted to explain that it was because of her, of what he felt for her, that he suddenly wanted so badly to be whole, to be alive. He had been sure she hadn't understood, but that afternoon on the path to the bathing shallows showed him something had survived. Berthe would have known he hadn't killed Plo-xlong. If she was simply waiting for him to tell her, then for him the world would open at that point.

"But you didn't tell her? You didn't say anything?"

Philip shook his head.

"Why?"

Philip didn't know. And the fact that he couldn't tell her grew heavier as they neared the water. She had held out salvation, freely asking only that he accept it. Once again he had hung up frozen at the moment of departure, and the chance had been lost.

Berthe had waited on the riverbank. A bright metallic blue butterfly danced out of the jungle toward her, the flat blades of its wings burning in the sunlight. She tried to get it to alight on her bathing towel; when she succeeded, she held it out toward him, her face glowing with pleasure. Philip knew that if he reached for it, it would be frightened away. He could only stand and watch it exercise its wings. He knew how far away he was from Berthe, how wide the gap was between their two worlds, and how unlikely it was such a distance could be closed.

He realized he had never wanted anything so clearly in his life—and, in the same instant, that he had never been quite so alone.

"Emotion comma human," the policeman began, but Philip interrupted him. He had failed to understand. The trip to the bathing shallows had been no accident. Philip knew the geologist often went with his daughter, ostensibly to guard her. That day was the first time he had been invited to join them. The geologist had a favorite spot between the roots of a strangler fig. From there he could see the edge of the women's section. He insisted that Philip sit with him, and as the boy did so, he felt the weight of the pistol in his pocket and knew what he would have to do.

"You didn't kill him."

Philip smiled. "You know, I almost threw it into the river. It was so stupid, the whole thing. But he sat there, chewing and snorting in the shade, and it was so damn hot I just sat there, too. I was staring at the glitter of the sun on the water, and I began to feel dizzy, almost nauseous. I hadn't slept for more than a day. I hadn't eaten. All the weight of everything was piling up in me, and I couldn't escape.

"Then he leaned on me, pressing me forward with his fat body and whispering something in my ear. I couldn't understand, but he kept doing it. He pushed me forward until I realized I could see Berthe, just beyond a row of bushes that grew into the water. He had known where she would be standing. He forced me forward, wheezing with the effort. She had her back toward us. Her body was so wet and smooth, but hard to look at because the sunlight was too bright. She began working on her elbows with the pumice stone. He was saying something, I couldn't tell what; then I understood that he wanted me to notice the way her breasts swayed as she scraped at her elbows.

"You think I didn't kill him? I shot that fat bastard!"

"You didn't do it."

"The setting sun was hanging in my face, hanging over the rim of the river, hanging over Berthe like an ax, dark orange and hollow—not at all like something burning, more like something about to be spilled . . .

"I was looking at it, staring at it. He told me to move closer so I could see better.

"I've just been too lonely. I've had friends, but still . . . Berthe . . . I knew I was going to try to make too much out of her. I could see I was going to try to make her be what I wanted, try to consume her in the same way . . . the same way . . ."

"Her father did her mother?"

"Yes. That's what I mean when I say lonely."

"But Berthe didn't feel that way?"

"I don't know."

"You probably don't."

"I don't think she understands."

"How do you know?"

"Because I could've waded out there and put my arms around her and what I'd have wanted would be the idea of doing that, the *idea* of it. And then if I'd done that,

214

after I'd done it, all I would have would be that I had had it."

The policeman gazed at his prisoner. He felt a growing desire to silence him, to get rid of him, to let him go back to his country and be done with him. There was no room here for such messiness. The boy was out of order.

"Because I could've pressed my face into Berthe's breasts and I know all I'd be doing would be thinking how here I was pressing my face into Berthe's breasts—and thinking about it."

"All right!" the policeman barked. "I don't think the investigation needs . . ."

"I mean there's something there, isn't there?"

"I don't want this. This is enough of this."

"And so I got out the pistol. And I still thought how I could think I was going to give it back to him. Except of course that wasn't true. From the very start, from the day I arrived upriver, it was always going to be easier to shoot him than to explain.

"So I shot him."

"No more," shouted the policeman.

"I shot him!"

"You can't have it!"

Philip glanced up at him, his lips curling into a smile. He pointed a single finger straight into the policeman's face. "I'll buy it," he declared. "And you know what I mean."

"I don't."

"Then you'll buy it."

"You think you can come here and, and . . ."

"You aren't your brother."

215

"Plo-xlong shot the geologist."

"Do you have to have it? That bad?"

The policeman's hands lifted up before his cheeks as if he wanted to scrape at the scar tissue. They closed into fists, then opened and dropped away. "Go home," he said. "Just go home."

"I am. But why don't you know me?"

◆《◆《◆《◆《◆《◆《◆《◆《

"Call Berthe Xlong."

The policeman stalked the back gallery of the court-room. He assured himself that everything was under control. Order would prevail. He counted a series of water stains on the wall. What else? Cracks split like lightning from the edge of the door? He stopped. His niece had taken the stand.

"You are Berthe Xlong?"

George Bates leaned forward, his forearms resting on his knees. Did he believe this was the critical moment? So it seemed. Detective Sergeant Xlong began pacing again. Had Mr. Bates noticed the alteration in his son? The boy appeared calm; there was to be no turning back.

Detective Sergeant Xlong's ears were ringing. He yawned self-consciously to clear them. The shouting in the streets was muted now. Were his men at last correctly applying the principles of crowd control that he had taught them? They had not taken to the lessons easily. Their natural juices flowed with the mob. Any variation in events immediately distracted them. Their reaction was always to surge.

Still, the policeman thought, it would be nice to be back in the barracks, sharing their cares, handing out assignments, giving advice.

He studied his niece on the stand and yawned again. Had he paid too much? But he had had no choice. No one carried him. Where was Moule? Dozing on her couch, probably, tangled in straps and pretending she was someplace else.

He stopped to examine the two soldiers he had placed beside the door. Their eyes were open but unfocused. Were they devious enough to sleep without closing their eyes? It was possible. They could be such a burden. If, as seemed likely, he lived for an unusually long time, credit would not be due to his men. So many times he had observed them hunched in their barracks, squandering an entire morning as each attempted to identify his own boots from the pile they had left the night before—guided solely by scent.

"How many?"

"I don't know. Many shots."

"More than five?" the judge asked, pleased with himself.

"Perhaps more than five. I don't remember."

"So we can assume the shots might have come from an automatic pistol rather than a revolver?"

The policeman clapped his palms against his face. Would this never end? He squeezed the ridges of scar tissue and applied pressure to his eyeballs. Why couldn't he stop yawning?

His Honor the judge was dragging it out, doing his best to prolong the questioning. The detective sergeant could scarcely bear it, but he knew the judge's resources were limited. That was a blessing. He wouldn't have the imagination to question Berthe on what she had been doing at the fatal moment. What if he asked her what she had been wearing? *Whoosh!* The policeman shuddered. *That* would stir the pot! They'd be here all day.

The judge droned on. He was so determined to make a display of his knowledge of firearms that he missed most of the real meat in the little scene at the riverbank. He launched into a recapitulation of Berthe's testimony, bungling the order of events sufficiently to cause even Berthe to gaze up at him in consternation.

Detective Sergeant Xlong groaned. He pressed his cheek against the cool back wall. The judge seemed about to begin once more at the beginning. That would be too much. The policeman stepped back and began slapping both palms loudly against the damp plaster. That helped. Silence filled the courtroom. That was better. He yawned again and resumed pacing. Now get on with it.

"Well, then," the judge said, blinking rapidly. "And you say you saw the man who shot your father?"

"Yes."

"Yes? Well, and you mean you saw him clearly?"

"Yes," Berthe replied.

"I see. And is that man here at the arraignment hearing?"

Good! Enough of that. Not another word. The policeman marched up the center aisle, swinging his arms, his boots resounding dully against the wet wood flooring.

Would Berthe have lied to save Philip? Her uncle assumed she would. Did she actually see the shooting? Probably not. Her back would have been turned. It didn't matter. Plo-xlong with a pistol in his hand. That was enough. If the truth didn't extend as far as one might wish, use something else. Plo-xlong shot the geologist. That was the way it was going to be. Plain and simple. Open and shut. He smiled to himself. Shut—a nice feeling.

The judge appeared to be disappointed that things had concluded so smoothly. He would have to make do with what he had. Detective Sergeant Xlong didn't bother to look at him. He was to dismiss the charges. He was to do it now.

Berthe stepped down, her eyes on Philip. Would he think she'd betrayed him? The policeman recognized that she, too, had crossed a frontier. It was left to Philip to decide. He was freed from the dock, but he didn't move. He remained motionless, silently returning Berthe's gaze.

Enough was enough. The detective sergeant advanced on the young foreigner. He snatched off his cap and thrust his face an inch from Philip's nose. His eyes narrowed; balls of sweat glistened in the grease on his forehead. He caught the boy's jaw in his fist and tilted his head up to meet him.

"You're free!" the policeman hissed. "Now you can go home!"

Philip said nothing. A cord of blood strummed beneath the skin of his temple. The policeman continued to peer into his face, but he could sense he was losing his concentration. Where were the burning buildings? Where were the coils of his people filing out through the silent river mists, funneling onto the single path that would end eventually in the automatic weapons of the invaders? And where was the voice of the teacher? And the lesson that to ensure adequate kindling, you were to first dynamite what you would burn?

Nothing. The policeman flexed his shoulders, reaching back for the most fundamental aid he'd ever recognized— and again found nothing, only the outlines of shadows. The dead really were gone from him.

And so here he held the face of this boy. And what was it reflected there? Was that longing? He released the jaw and eased himself back. His niece had altered Philip; she had forced him to live in the world. Yet the policeman himself had continued to think of Berthe as only a child— hadn't he been wrong?

"Go home," the policeman repeated, his voice dropping to a whisper. Philip returned his stare now, but with little of his previous aggressiveness.

"You still don't understand, do you?" the boy said.

"No."

He replaced his cap. He seated the edge of the visor against the familiar groove in his forehead. Did he feel better? The bailiff was ordered to clear the court. A few spectators began to protest, but the policeman ignored them. He wanted it over. He wanted everyone to go home.

Berthe waited behind him. Where should she go? He turned to look at her but didn't reply. Now George Bates was behind him. He was saying something. Philip was there, also waiting for him.

"What do you want?" the policeman asked.

"Listen," George Bates interrupted. "He doesn't know what he wants. Let's save this for another time."

"How do you know I don't know what I want?"

The policeman glanced at his niece. Her arms were folded over her breasts; her face was calm. He had seen his sister stand like that. Did that mean Berthe was a woman? He had no idea. What did Philip want with her? He had no way of knowing. He himself had wanted people to be quiet. He had wanted them to leave, or to come, or to speak, or confess, or sit up straight, or listen while he spoke, or fetch something, but beyond that—nothing.

"He said we could go, Philip."

"Why did you come here for me?"

"Don't you realize how worried I've been? How much trouble I've . . . ?"

"You were that sure I couldn't take care of myself?"

"Philip, we can go!"

"So you thought you could help me. But what if I didn't want you to help me?"

"We can go now."

"Don't I have that right?"

"Can't we talk about this later?"

"Can't we talk about it now?"

"Whatever you want."

"Maybe I don't want to talk about it at all."

"Fine."

"Would you like that?"

"Whatever you want."

"It wouldn't surprise you if I didn't want to talk about it?"

"Philip . . ."

"You told me about a son respecting his father. When does that turn around? When does the father respect the son?"

"If you don't want to talk about it now, that's fine."

"Why do you think it's me who doesn't want to talk about it?"

"Well, why do you think it was that I didn't respect you?"

"That wasn't what it was?"

"Or that you didn't respect yourself?"

"How could I respect myself when you didn't respect me?"

"I don't think I didn't respect you. I think you thought I didn't respect you, so you couldn't respect yourself."

"Maybe. But if you respected me, then why did I think you didn't?"

"I don't know. I guess I didn't know how to say anything like how I respected you because I was afraid you would think I didn't know how to talk to you because I didn't respect you."

"Well, maybe. But don't you think I thought you thought I knew what you were thinking?"

"I don't know," George Bates admitted slowly. "I guess I assumed you thought I thought you assumed what I was thinking without so much thinking what you assumed I thought . . ."

Detective Sergeant Xlong raised one arm, but no one noticed. He turned toward his niece. Had she, too, felt the earth gape open beneath their feet? Apparently she had not. Her face was as calm as a pool on a day without weather. Years in the police had left him wary. Was it inexperience that made her unaware of the appalling nature of the foreigners' groping? He squared his pistol belt. It was uncomfortable to think that his niece wasn't with him.

Philip explained that everything he had was his because his father gave it to him. But since his father gave it to him, he always had the feeling it wasn't really his.

But his father had wanted him to have what he himself hadn't had.

Granted. But that wasn't what Philip felt he had been given.

His father didn't understand. Neither did the policeman.

Philip said that he had been given what his father had gotten, not what his father had had.

His father still didn't understand. The policeman attempted to turn his own attention toward some water stains on the ceiling he'd never noticed before.

Philip explained that as what he had been given was what his father had gotten, he never had anything, as he never actually had the opportunity to have the capacity to get anything to give.

"Oh," the father said. The policeman counted the stains. There were only four, but he counted them again.

The boy pointed out that as what he had was what he had been given and thus not his, he felt he must not deserve it, and as he didn't deserve it, it thus could never be his, and therefore as the amount of gifts he couldn't have mounted, the number of those he might conceivably have diminished correlatively—that is, of a coefficient of one to one—and so, as this process continued, necessarily did the possibility of his arriving at a sufficient plane of self-worth to deal effectively with the mass of objects, events, and cases he found himself surrounded by to the degree that he might, as it were, own something.

"Oh."

One of the stains, the most elongated, could be thought of, in dim light, as actually being two. Thus, the detective sergeant realized, the total could as well be thought of as five. Or, he concluded to himself, one more than four.

"Yes, ungrateful, and because . . ."

"Yes, ungrateful, and I never knew but I supposed . . ."

"Yes . . ."

"Yes."

Berthe looked at each of them. She said she was hungry.

❖❰❖❰❖❰❖❰❖❰❖❰❖❰❖❰

Here was a bitter moment. This must be what they meant when they said sad. The floors were hollow, the walls drained of color. Moule had left the massage table, but her personal belongings were gone. The detective sergeant squatted in a corner and stared about him. The sky beyond her windows glowed violet as an old bruise. What was he supposed to do?

He thought of his brother, lashing himself through the wet forest. Had his men deserted him yet? It was only a matter of time. His most recent failure would be insurmountable. Poor Plo-xlong. He would be reduced to his programs, stripped down to the language of his slogans. Could he have sincerely hoped to take over the smeltery? It was never to have been his. To the degree that he searched for it in material goods, he mistook his legacy. You didn't have what you had, the policeman knew; you had what you could apply—particularly in the face of dissension.

So was it over? And what was he to do? Without pirates on the river, the police might turn in upon themselves, turn inward to suck at their own wounds and in the process wither, curl, shrink away.

The floor was gray; the streets below thickened with evening, causing the paper Moule had glued to her walls to swell in the twilight green of rain. Philip was the true heir; the geologist had perhaps recognized it immediately. He might have even realized that there could be no real transmission, and that Philip's heritage was to be the geologist's own death—set up by the boy's failure to kill Plo-xlong. What could he have gotten from that? The policeman had no idea. But he suspected one thing. The geologist had underestimated his own daughter. Berthe was now clearly in control in a way her mother had never managed to be.

Detective Sergeant Xlong climbed up onto the massage table. He lay on his stomach. The wood felt smooth and dry, but it was lonely on a massage table by yourself, too lonely. Had he made some sort of mistake? Beyond his occasional excessive explanations, he had been rather mild with Moule. He had asked very little of her, hardly more than her hands and time. Why had he been abandoned?

Berthe had taken him aside as they left the courtroom. He was to understand what would be required of him. Berthe was going to live, but first she would bury her dead—*all* her dead. He hadn't understood; she declined to explain. But the following day he would be obliged to conduct Mr. Bates and his son upriver. Was she asking?

Was this a favor begged from a favorite uncle? She smiled, but shook her head. He was a policeman; it was his responsibility. Philip had to finish what he'd begun. She'd wait for them in town.

In the streets beyond the window, he could hear the cooing voices of women as they strolled back from bathing in the river. This hour they had selected for their pleasure was the time he most often felt the yearning for what he labeled "Companionship comma Human." Now, alone on the dry massage table, he squeezed into himself, gripping the edges with his fists and forcing himself to spread open to the insistent blood thudding him home.

Beneath him, the women of the town ambled past in indolent groups. They drew teak combs through their glossy hair and brushed gently against each other the way they did every evening.

He was a policeman. There was no moment he was not on duty. His body kneaded itself against the dry wood; going home, he thought to himself, going home again.

The insides of the fingers, the palms and wrists of the passing women would be white in the moonlight, languorous as the peeled throats of snakes. Berthe had said tomorrow they were going home—going, the word filled him with blood. He could hear the voices of the women singing. They were chanting verses from a hymn which celebrated the ecstatic copulations of cow-herding maidens with their blue-skinned boy god. He pressed his eyes closed tightly to hear better. He was going home tomorrow—and going now, faster, feeling a stroke of affection returned from the dry wood of the table.

The policeman knew how familiar the ankles of the

women were with water, how the hairs on the insides of their thighs rose up amorously at the touch of the river's fingers—he knew, he knew, but it didn't seem to apply to him. He was going. He had understood how the smeltery had begun as nothing more than a gift to his sister; how it had been the true product of her union with the geologist; and how, as that union foundered, it was altered and became the poison that her husband fed upon. He had always known this, and he was going.

The promenade of women continued beneath the darkened room. A single soprano would direct the aimless melody for a few bars before being joined by a chorus of contraltos. Did they suspect he was up here? It seemed unlikely. Might they be singing for him? No, they were singing for themselves. And he, too, by himself, was going, going home.

His sister's first baby had been born dead; the geologist had turned toward his smeltery in pain. A second child lived for several weeks before it too died. The geologist buried his grief in the hoard of tin he had refined. Even when after years of trying he was presented with a child that lived, he could not cross back to her. He had become his smeltery. He held his little daughter, but she had no reality for him. He had come to depend upon tin, and the hatred of his enemies.

The policeman on his table going knew how the geologist had loved. He had followed him, memorized him, married him as firmly as had his sister—and he was going. Why had the geologist sent Philip after Plo-xlong? Going now, going home. Because he knew the boy could never pull the trigger. Why had he wanted the pressure applied?

227

Going, going. Because the geologist had nothing left, nothing more he wanted beyond his coming fusion with Plo-xlong—his suicide.

Gone, then, he was home, home here. The boy running through the night jungle was hardly more than a messenger, a spasm shaken from the past. Gone, he breathed. Gone again. Only when the boy hadn't shot had he begun to be a man—his gift from the geologist, his wedding present, and one Berthe had recognized clearly.

Gone, alone, abandoned, he arrived at his final question—why Plo-xlong? Why had *he*, the policeman, never been chosen, not even for the final act, the final brick? Why had the geologist chosen Plo-xlong for his mating with death?

Slack on the table, the policeman had no answer. He would fill again, he knew. He would be back. It was his habit at moments just past pain to count his blessings, to roll in the fact that once again it had only been a flesh wound, that once again there was so little visible damage, so little lost.

He thought of Philip standing on the riverbank with the loaded pistol in his hand and the second chance before him. Plo-xlong had stepped out of his ambush, perhaps not quite able to believe he had ended his struggle at last. The policeman blinked. Red stars of blood flashed behind his eyelids—Philip hadn't shot. Was it Berthe bent over her father? Perhaps. Had the lips and cheekbones of his niece saved his younger brother's life? It seemed likely.

He sagged, once again passed out of himself and at ease in his uniform. He was a policeman. He knew the women swung their hips as they walked, but it wasn't for him.

Their dark nipples trembled with the soft weight of breasts released from daylight wrappers. He knew how their swinging hems were weighted with tiny bits of pure tin, holding the gauzy fabric against their thighs—but it wasn't for him, wasn't for the police. He knew how their fingertips followed down the sweep of bellies, gentle as coins minted from the mantles of clams, stroking toward the fish each carried—he knew, but it simply wasn't to be for him.

five ⬦≼⬦≼⬦≼⬦≼⬦≼⬦≼⬦≼⬦≼⬦≼⬦≼⬦≼⬦≼⬦≼⬦≼⬦

"No!"

Sprague's leg was bound with black plastic tape. He held an automatic rifle in his hands.

"This here's private property!"

Soldiers snuffled at the prospect of a shoot-out. The policeman could sense their fingers crawling toward triggers. He stepped forward. Sprague should realize they had not come to arrest him.

"Then get off my smeltery!"

Detective Sergeant Xlong would have said they only came to bury the dead, but Philip anticipated him. He strode forward, ignoring Sprague's threats. They had been down to the bathing shallows. There was no sign of the corpse. Of course they didn't intend to accuse Sprague of anything. They simply needed information.

"You think I stole it?"

Philip said they thought nothing of the kind.

"Something could've ate it, you know."

Philip smiled. The detective sergeant began to comment, but Sprague interrupted him.

"A thing like that! I didn't take it. What would I want with it?"

Philip explained that that was the very question which was puzzling them.

"I'll tell you what's puzzling me is why you're in with that cop! That's what's puzzling me."

Philip shrugged. He glanced for a moment at the detective sergeant. If there was still a degree of friction between them, the boy no longer seemed to be concerned with it. The policeman had the odd sensation of the afternoon draining away through his fingers like grains of dry sand. He wondered if he shouldn't step forward and insert himself; but before he could decide, Philip resumed the questioning.

Would it be possible that some of the people who worked at the smeltery might know something?

"Work? Those lazy goddamn . . ."

Granted. Philip raised his hands. He'd been here. Work was not the word. He could appreciate Sprague's disappointment. He, too, had been surprised by the dilapidated condition of the smeltery. He had suspected sabotage, but there was little evidence of such an intention. It was only neglect. The physical plant had been reduced to little more than a rusting heap of useless machinery.

"Nothing works," Sprague cried. "I've been trying. You couldn't even sell it for scrap!"

Perhaps, Philip agreed. But was he so certain the smeltery was beyond salvation?

Sprague watched him without comment. Philip stripped the vines away from one of the rock crushers. The rubber fittings and belts had rotted; they would have to be replaced. But the rusted parts could be unfrozen; penetrating oil might loosen them enough to disassemble. Some of the buildings would have to be replaced; but once cleaned out, the furnaces could be fired; the boy was certain of it. Once they got a crew together, they'd be no more than a couple of months away from production.

"He owed *me*," Sprague said defensively. Philip just smiled. "How'm I going to know you aren't going to rip me off just like he did?"

"You can't."

"Then I wouldn't have a damn thing . . ."

"What have you got now?"

Sprague looked around him. Even if he managed to cut back the jungle and repair the equipment, he could never get the operation going by himself.

"He *owed* me, you know?"

"Sure."

"Him and his old lady. What do you think it was like? Sitting here slaving while they were rolling all over each other!"

"So what did you do with the body?"

"I didn't kill him!"

"Nobody said you did."

"Hell, you were there yourself!"

Philip shrugged, but said nothing.

"You can't pin it on me."

"The body," Philip insisted.

"How come you want it so much?"

The policeman had loosened his clothing. His cap was shoved to the back of his head, his hands were empty. This talking was messy. It was better when one cut through to the bone. He was a policeman; he should have been involved from the start. He had given the boy room to maneuver. That, apparently, had been a mistake. Philip was going too far.

He stepped forward. "No." Sprague glowered. "Stay back." The policeman ignored him. He stopped next to Philip and draped a heavy arm around the boy's shoulders in a manner he assumed would appear avuncular. He informed him that if he tried to rebuild the smeltery for himself, he would be dead within a month.

Philip paled, but he didn't back off. This was a business deal, pure and simple. No laws were being broken here. Once the coroner's inquest was completed, he would be having nothing further to do with the detective sergeant.

"And Berthe? Nothing further to do with my niece?"

"Dead within a month," Philip countered. "At whose hands, yours?"

They stared at each other. Philip declared that he would not be threatened and he would not be baited. And as for Berthe, he didn't even want to hear her name in the detective sergeant's mouth.

"And Berthe's mother? You will have nothing to say to Berthe's mother? But I'm afraid you are underestimating the bonds that attach us. It might be time to take a moment and reflect upon who you are and what you can . . ."

"No," Philip interrupted, "upon who you are."

The policeman didn't understand.

"What do you think I'm buying?"

The body was their currency, granted; they recognized that in each other. But the boy still failed to assess the situation correctly. The policeman turned and placed the meat of his palm against the boy's cheek. "You can't buy my niece," he said, patting him.

Philip seized his wrist in both hands and forced it down. "I don't have to buy her."

"What do you mean?"

"You know what I mean."

"Then who do you think you're buying?"

Philip still held the policeman's wrist. He raised the man's hand, twisting it back until he had positioned the scarred fingers before the detective sergeant's parted lips.

"You," Philip said, and shoved.

The policeman jerked back, his boot heel catching on an exposed root. He grabbed one of his soldiers to keep himself from falling.

"You don't *touch* the police!" he cried, his voice cracking.

"Nor do you buy them," Philip added. "But you do. You do—and you know it."

The policeman glared at the boy without replying. He had regained his balance. His face was hot. Was he going to have an attack? Evidently not. He glanced up at the sky. White clouds sailed past. Where was the next storm? It didn't even look like it was about to rain soon. What was he to do?

He laced his fingers, reversed his hands, and cracked his knuckles. Untouchable, *whoosh!* Never better than when under fire. Rise to the occasion. Reach back for that extra, extra, extra . . . where was what he thought of as the weather? Where were the distractions that soothed him? Places, things in them, one and one and one. And, and, and . . . where were the explanations he had packed against his wounds? Where were the lips of trees? The green fingers of water that stroked him, stroked him, stroked him? Gone here, gone now. Was he to be reduced to his thumb? Not yet! He clutched himself. Damaged, but he was a man—he would be, be, be felt!

He drew his pistol and cocked back the hammer.

"No." George Bates groaned.

The policeman stepped up and put the muzzle against Philip's temple. "Now," he said, his voice coming from far away. "Everyone watch me."

"Okay," Sprague cried suddenly. "I got it. Hell, I was going to give it to you. Don't do nothing!"

The policeman blinked. Sprague rushed on, talking fast.

"Hell, by the time I'd found it the crabs had been at it like they do, you know; so it wasn't exactly what you'd call a valuable piece of . . . whatever—property? No, not property. I mean it didn't *look* like much. But I thought how, now, hell, I'm never going to get mine back unless I get it out of that—meaning him, you understand."

The policeman nodded.

"So I got right after it. Damn, if it didn't take most of the night. It was so heavy and me with a bum leg and all. I almost gave it up. I had ropes and roller logs and a pulley—except it hadn't been lubricated in about ten years and so wasn't worth much—which is how it is around here—everything all beat up and left out in the rain and not maintained. Hell, he threw away stuff I couldn't even afford to buy. How do you think that made me feel? You know?"

The policeman nodded again. The pistol had come down. Philip released a sigh so deep that he began coughing at the end. He tried to catch his breath but couldn't. He doubled over, gagging. The detective sergeant began pounding his back mechanically, staring with a listless gaze at the trees behind them.

"Hell." Sprague laughed, rushing forward again. "I yelled at that body. 'You're paying!' I yelled. 'I'm going to get it out of you!' Damn, but I about had a fit, trying to drag him someplace he'd be more than a free meal.

"You think I had any help? Hell, no! I've never had any. That's the way it's always been for me. He'd say, 'C. K., handle this for me.' And I'd be up on that slope breaking my butt while he'd be down on the riverbank, making his old lady squeal, rolling around stinking up the jungle. Hell, if he and his old lady hadn't broken up, we never would have gotten the tin production business up where it'd be worth anybody's time. Not that it is now, mind you. You know?"

George Bates nodded.

"I had to truss on the arms with binder's twine because they kept getting hooked up on every little damn bush. And the whole thing was so slippery you couldn't hardly get a proper hold on it. And it was dark. And it was so bad-smelling sometimes I'd wonder if it was such a good idea. I mean, there were these loose pieces coming off; and the head was loose, too, what with the water, and the crabs all chewing for free, and who knows what, you know? I mean, if the head came off, then the rest of the thing wouldn't have much value, not that it had that much anyway, other than as a kind of curiosity piece, like they say. I sure had my doubts. I'd stop and I'd look at it and I'd think to myself: C. K., you sure you aren't making a mistake? And myself would think back: Well, one thing, you lose much more of it and it sure as hell will be what you would call depreciated. You know?"

Nobody nodded this time.

"But where is it?" Philip said.

"I'm getting to that. I figured I could use it as a kind of lever to get myself worked back into the tin production business. I figured I could use it on Plo-xlong long enough to get this place cleaned up and going again. I didn't know what it was like here until afterwards. When I got up here I realized it was going to take a lot more than just one corpse, big as he was. I mean, you could have a hundred of them lined up head to heels and that still wouldn't get you enough momentum to get this place going. You know?"

"But where is it?"

"Damn! Whenever anything gets down to being mine, it's just because it's so beat-up nobody else would have it!"

"It's not here?"

Sprague's jaw was set. He shook his head. He wasn't exactly sure what had happened. He said he'd sort of misplaced it.

"Misplaced it?"

"Easy come, easy go?"

Philip glanced at the policeman. The pistol still hung from his fist. Detective Sergeant Xlong turned toward the boy. He slapped himself in the face with his free hand and shook his head, trying to gather his concentration. He realized what the boy was looking at and self-consciously slipped it back into its holster.

"No corpse, then?" the policeman ventured and smiled. His voice was firm; the boy would have to be feeling reassured. He was the protector again—the man with a badge who stepped up and took charge. This was a good world, a very good world. And as he had always insisted, he was the true father.

He tugged at his lower lip, dragging it down from his teeth. Although it was true that communication between humans was imperfect, that was no reason to abandon it. He released his lip. He would be forgiven his display of bad temper, and he himself in turn would gratefully accept this forgiveness. The world pulsed back and forth, he mused peacefully. What obtained was change. The dead became the living and the living became the dead. One twisted one's fingers into a loose flap of skin—and felt the torque pass through one's own body as well as through that of the other.

Yes, well, now to the business at hand. Sprague stared at him; he would take the man in his own terms. Philip's moment of boldness would lead to others. No problem. The boy would soon be family. And George Bates? He too would have his corner.

"So, no corpse, then?" The policeman understood that his body was unending. Every flea, every louse, every bit of moss clinging to the unlit quarters of his groin rode as a testimony; every spore and seed that dropped away, every egg from every parasite was his, all was him, his expansion. He felt hookworms enter through the soles of his feet, felt lung flukes cut their crooked paths, felt roundworms, pinworms, tapeworms, felt every kind of jungle spirochete skip, slither, wriggle, or hop up for his blessing, up to accept his wet flesh as host, as living host, loving host.

"No corpse?" But they would understand that he was his configurations; he would be his phases. Moule was gone; he would stroke through her memory for years. He understood that his face was massed with clouds. He knew his hair was filled with stars. He was a policeman. He would guarantee the sun's setting to the identical world it arose to. The days would follow each other as orderly as prisoners. There was only one truth, and it was counting. Within this he would encase himself. One finger, two fingers, three, four, a fist! *Whoosh!* Here was the perfect pleasure of the police.

"Now," he said, "this is what we'll do."

❖❖❖❖❖❖❖❖❖❖❖

His sister sat hunched beside her low fire and refused to speak. She had become so old. Her hair was streaked with gray; there was no shine to it. If she was surprised that her brother would conduct the two foreigners in to see her, she gave no indication. There was no color to her. She didn't seem to be bitter so much as simply empty. The policeman assumed she was grieving for her lost husband, without, however, losing sight of the fact that she herself was almost surely the source of his death.

Rain tore at the flimsy walls of the longhouse. The wet

bamboo slapped and shuddered as the rain leaked through the roof in a dozen places. His sister's cooking fire smoldered from the wetness. Sitting beside it, George Bates and his son would feel no warmth. Their clothing would never dry. The detective sergeant knew that their skins, like his, would come to maintain the oily moistness of those who make their homes too near fish.

"And what about Berthe?" the policeman demanded in a firm voice. "Is your daughter to rot here, too?"

Mr. Bates might have argued that the disaster of the first generation did not necessarily guarantee that of the second—or that even if it did, that, too, could be acceptable. Unfortunately, at the moment he also seemed to have nothing to say.

The policeman sighed and stood to search for dry wood. No one helped him. He would have enjoyed a moment of conversation with his sister. He would have enjoyed reliving the past, but she refused. He broke strips of bamboo from one of the inner walls; they were as damp as the rest of the structure. The decay was total. The building would never survive the next monsoon season.

"Your daughter's a woman," the detective sergeant said in a loud voice. Nothing; she stared at the fire, her fists buried in a pile of rags she had been mending when they arrived. "It's not like it was," he added in their dialect, causing her to raise her eyes toward him for the first time. "She's changed. She belongs in town."

"Changed?" his sister echoed, her voice still not taking on anger; just hollow.

The policeman nodded, then turned to tear out another section of wall. He had suddenly remembered how her husband used to press himself on her, clawing at her, shaking his yellow hair as he pried at her thighs. After he had coupled with her, he would pull back and stare at her and tell her she must never change. She was never to move. When the first baby died, his sister believed it was because she hadn't been what he wanted. She begged him to forgive her; she couldn't understand what he wanted. She tried to please him. But when the second baby died, he turned away from her. She pleaded with him to come back to the riverbank. She would try to be whatever he wanted her to be. He said he didn't want her to be anything. He wouldn't look at her. He said he had to plan for the future; he sat at his desk, studying smeltery figures.

When Berthe didn't die, she had thought he would come back to her. The baby was strong. Everyone in the kampong waited for him to be more at ease, to become playful again. It didn't happen. He didn't have anything to say to her. Finally, after weeks of silence, she forced her way into his office. She held out the baby and demanded that he speak to her.

"Look at your daughter," she told him. "She's alive!"

He looked, but it didn't seem to have any meaning for him.

"What do you want?"

"More tin," he said simply; and she knew he meant it.

Her work took on fury; there was nothing for her to vent her bitterness on except the ore brought out of the jungle. He had become his smeltery; she had no choice but to join him. Together, they smelted tin.

His sister's gaze returned to the fire. She had made her own choices. The policeman understood that her daughter would be allowed to do the same. Berthe would take Philip up and make something out of him; but not here, and not at the smeltery, and perhaps not even in the Republic.

All the bamboo in the room was useless. He checked the lattice before the passageway; it was also soaked.

Where would they go? Singapore? Hong Kong? What if everyone left at once? It would be quieter, neater; he would enjoy that. He glanced back at his sister. George Bates was explaining something to her. She ignored him, but the policeman suspected she would be listening.

He moved down through the broken galleries of his childhood home, avoiding the holes opened in the bamboo floor. A section of wall collapsed with a wet crash as he passed, and the rain blew in on him, green with fury, exploding leaves lashing against smashed bamboo splinters.

The deepest wing of the longhouse had been abandoned first, for it had always touched directly into the ribs of the jungle. Even when the Xlong brothers were boys, this area had been considered haunted. The lattices were all broken, and most of the ceiling and floor were gone, so the rain drove through as freely as river water passing a wicker fish trap. The jungle had grown in over the back edge of this frame and covered a third of the room.

On the single section of floor still remaining, so covered with mold as to be completely featureless, lay the swollen body of the rogue geologist. There was a phosphorescent glow about him in the rain light, like a freshly plowed mountain covered with the green of young plants. Tendrils had found his legs; and if he remained undisturbed, he, too, would soon be swallowed by the jungle.

A single vulture was perched on a broken window beam, gazing at the policeman with reptilian stupidity. He slowly drew his pistol. Its feathers were soaked and its head was hunched; yet it had no sense of misery—nor, judging by the unbroken curve of the hill that had been the geologist, did it have much hunger.

It just sat there, settled in itself. The policeman cocked back the hammer on his pistol. He stared at the wet skin covering the deformed skull of the bird, the color like the belly-up dead whiteness of poisoned fish. He searched in himself for some emotion, something to label, to say this was what it was—and found nothing. He was whatever he had become—a man of technique, a man who had little need to ask the difficult questions when the simple ones seemed to fill the world with sufficient awe. Well, good enough. He would be it.

He held his pistol out at arm's length. He aimed at the blood-red jewel of the bird's eye. It observed him without fear, without curiosity; it sat simply folded into its stupidity.

The vulture did not fill him with rage. He was not planning to shoot it as a parting tribute to his dead adversary. This was not to be a gesture in honor of the man he had followed, learned from, hated—his spiritual father, his teacher. No, this was to be a pure shooting, a simple act of organization: a subtraction—one less.

But as his finger closed on the trigger, he caught sight of his younger brother crouched in the jungle beyond. Plo-xlong clutched his rifle against his body to protect it against the storm, his face green and streaming with rain.

Poor Plo-xlong was waiting for them to go away. He was

243

waiting for them to relinquish the hopeless scrap of fire, the dry spot beside his sister, the few hungers that could still distinguish him from the vulture.

Their eyes met. They exchanged glances only brothers could know—a perfect transfer of information: the rifle would be loaded, the pistol was cocked; it would be such a simple thing to bring the world crashing down upon them and end the moment.

But the policeman knew that they would not. And the vulture, too, would die on another day. The elder brother replaced the pistol in its holster. Did his sister have the geologist killed because she knew he was dying? Had she needed revenge that badly? Plo-xlong's night under Philip's pistol would have been enough to put him in motion, but his sister must have been the one to decide that it was time. Had she been too full of rage? Or had she simply recognized that her husband was ready to die, and aided him in the only way she could?

The policeman didn't know. He could see he would find a comfortable balance against Sprague, although it would be difficult for them to involve others without some form of industrial production. Perhaps Philip was right, and the machinery could be repaired. He had no idea.

The violence of the squall suddenly increased. Trees whipped against the black sky, and sheets of rain bounced and blew in every direction. The river would flood, the policeman knew. Much of their crop would be destroyed —it happened every time. It was what you knew if you lived in the jungle.

He wondered if he could ask his sister about the decision to shoot the geologist. He felt a moment of affection for her, mostly because she was not in sight. Nor was Moule, he thought pleasurably, aware that his memories were intact. Tonight he would spend thirty minutes thinking about Moule. Nothing could take that away.

Plo-xlong had found shelter beneath some wide leaves, although they did him no more good than the wreck of their longhouse did the policeman. Plo-xlong squatted down, tucked himself in, and closed his eyes to wait. He would know that the pursuit of the police would once again become haphazard. He would know where he could be.

And the policeman, as he turned to rejoin his guests, what did he know? He knew the blink in the vulture's eye. He knew the green of the rain and the brown of the river. He knew he himself would no doubt live on and on and on.

And he knew the investigation would always be the responsibility of the members of the police.